WRANGLING A LUCKY COWBOY

Copyright © February 2024 by Katie Lane

Cover Design and Interior Format

Wrangling a
LUCKY
COWBOY

HOLIDAY
RANCH
TWO

KATIE LANE

To Margie Hager,
Book lover, author supporter, kindest soul,
and dear friend.
I miss you, Sweet Pea

CHAPTER ONE

ROME REMINGTON NEVER thought he'd find himself standing in front of the altar again. He was a man who learned from his mistakes. After his first failed attempt at marriage, he had no intentions of entering the holy bond of matrimony a second time. No matter how much his father was pushing for grandkids to carry on the Remington name.

Rome had spent his life fulfilling his father's wishes. While other kids rode bikes and played video games after school, he'd studied for hours so he could hand Sam Remington a report card filled with As. In high school, he'd gone out for the football team regardless of the fact that he hated football. In college, he'd majored in business, even though he'd wanted to major in animal science. Once he'd graduated and returned home, he'd searched for the right woman to marry—one his father would approve of.

He still wanted to please his dad. But he wasn't willing to tie the knot again. He figured it was time for his little brother to step up to the plate and take one for the Remington team. Casey certainly had no trouble getting women to fall in love with him. Half of the female population of Wilder, Texas, was trying to win his heart.

Rome understood why. Casey had a good heart. Rome's was a little too battle scarred. Which was why he had no intentions of offering it again. Thankfully, he wasn't the one exchanging vows today.

But that didn't seem to stop him from sweating through his tuxedo as he listened to Decker and Sweetie exchange vows. Knots the size of Brahman bull balls grew in his stomach as memories swirled to life in his head. Memories of the sweet timbre of Emily's voice when she promised to love, honor, and cherish him forever. The teasing sparkle of her blue eyes when he lifted the thin wisp of her veil to kiss her. The welcoming softness of her lips. The tight grip of her hand on his arm as if she never wanted to let him go.

She had let him go.

Eighteen months later, she had packed up and headed back to Georgia, teaching him that love was a fickle and untrustworthy emotion he wanted no part of.

"Rome?"

He blinked back to the present moment and found Decker holding out his hand and giving him a quizzical look. Rome quickly slipped his hand in his pants pocket and pulled out the rings. Unfortunately, when he went to hand them to Decker, one slipped from his shaky fingers and bounced down the steps of the dais. As he moved down the steps to retrieve it, he could feel everyone's eyes on him.

He should be used to people's attention. As sons of one of the wealthiest ranchers in Texas, he and Casey had always known the townsfolk had high expectations of them. Casey let those expectations roll right off his back and did exactly what he pleased. Rome couldn't do that. There was something inside him that desperately wanted to meet those expectations. Everyone's expectations. The townsfolk's, his father's . . . his wife's.

He had failed.

When the ceremony ended and the preacher declared Decker and Sweetie man and wife, that failure punched Rome hard in the chest and he found himself in a full-fledged panic attack. His vision blurred, his heart started thumping like crazy, and he couldn't seem to pull a full breath into his lungs.

Decker and Sweetie started down the aisle to a loud round of applause. As the best man, Rome knew he was supposed to follow. But he was struggling just to stay standing. There was no way he could put one foot in front of the other.

Then a cool hand slid into his and gripped it firmly.

He held tightly to the lifeline he'd been given and allowed himself to be led down the aisle and out of the barn. He barely registered the stiff February breeze as he was pulled around the side of the barn.

"Sit." Firm pressure was applied to his shoulders and his legs finally gave out. His butt had barely landed on a stack of firewood when his black Stetson was whisked off and his head pushed down to his knees. "Breathe."

It took a few wheezy tries before his lungs started to partially fill. When the spots lifted from his vision, he found himself looking at two sets of cowboy boots. His own black size thirteens and a much smaller red pair. There was only one person who had worn red boots to the wedding. Sweet-ie's boots were white. All four of the bridesmaids' boots were pink. Only the maid of honor wore red. And Rome would bet money that the color hadn't been her choice.

Clover Fields Holiday was not a bold red kind of person, even though she carried the surname of her mama's side of the family. Fanny Fields had run the very first house of ill repute in the county. Mrs. Fields's Boardinghouse wasn't as notorious as the infamous Chicken Ranch, but the wild things that had gone on in the house were how the town of Wilder had gotten its name. All the boys in school had often discussed which Holiday sister had taken after her mama's side of the family.

Cloe's name had never come up.

She was the reserved wallflower of the six Holiday sisters. The one who stood back and watched instead of participating. She wasn't the popular Miss Soybean like her oldest sister, Sweetheart. Or a smart bookworm like her middle sister, Belle. Nor was she an overachiever like Belle's twin, Liberty. She wasn't an athletic cowgirl like her next to the youngest sister, Halloween. Or a bouncy cheerleader like her youngest sister, Noelle.

She was just Cloe, a girl who didn't seem to waste her time trying to prove herself.

Unlike Rome.

Even now he felt like he had to prove he was fine by sitting up—even when doing so made him feel lightheaded and dizzy. When he finally focused, he discovered the familiar girl he had known most of his life staring back at him.

Cloe was only a few inches under Rome's six feet one inches and skinny as a willow branch. She always wore clothes that looked two sizes too big. Even the maid of honor's dress hung well past her knees. While her sisters either had their daddy's blond or their mama's black hair, Cloe's hair was the brownish-red color of autumn leaves right before they drop to the ground. Although it was hard to tell the true color when she always kept it confined in clips or twisty buns. Today, it was fixed on top of her head in a tower of curls that tilted to one side like a lopsided fence post.

Like the rest of her sisters, she'd gotten her mama's pretty green eyes. While most people started using contacts in high school, Cloe continued to wear glasses that always seemed to be slipping down the bridge of her button nose. Like now. Instead of pushing them up with her hand, she wrinkled her nose until they slid back into place as she continued to fan him with the hat.

"Concentrate on taking deep, even breaths," she said. "The only way to get through a panic attack is to regulate your breathing."

The fact she knew he was having a panic attack made him even more panicked. If word got out it would spread like wildfire and everyone would think he was still upset over Emily leaving. He wasn't. He damn well wasn't.

"I'm not having a panic attack. It was just hot in the barn." Considering it was the middle of February and most people in attendance were wearing jackets, it was a weak excuse. He tried to get to his feet to prove he was okay, but when everything spun again, he was forced to sit back down and put his head between his knees. Which annoyed him and made him a little snappish.

"Look, I'm fine. I just need a few minutes . . . alone."

The red boots didn't move, but the fanning stopped and she lowered his hat. There was something about the sight of her hand cradling the crown of his black Stetson that grabbed his attention. Her fingers were long and slender, the nails neatly trimmed and devoid of polish. Emily had kept her nails lengthy and painted bright colors. She couldn't open Coke cans and got upset when one chipped or broke off. While those manicured nails had been sexy as hell, he'd always worried about being impaled when she handled his man parts. That wouldn't be a problem with Cloe. Those long fingers could easily wrap around his—

Whoa, boy!

He brought a screeching halt to the thought train that had completely run off the rails. Obviously, his three-year dry spell had finally caught up with him. Cloe Holiday giving him a hand job? What was the matter with him? Shock at his wayward thoughts gave him the jolt he needed to regulate his breathing and sit up.

Her eyes behind the lenses were filled with concern and kindness. Which made him feel badly about being so snappish.

"Sorry I'm being a bear. Weddings aren't really my thing."

She smiled softly. She had a nice smile. It wasn't fake or too big. It was just . . . nice.

"Weddings are stressful, aren't they? Not only for the bride and groom, who feel like they are the hosts, but also for their parents who are watching their money leak down the drain. Then there are the bachelors who fear their girlfriends will get marriage fever and start demanding proposals. And their girlfriends who are stressed because they're worried they won't ever get that proposal." Her smile faded. "And finally there are the people who have gambled at love and lost. For those people, weddings just make them feel like . . . complete and utter failures."

Cloe had hit the nail right on the head. Rome felt like a complete and utter failure. He just wasn't willing to admit it. Especially when she was giving him that pitying look. Sympathy was not something Remingtons had ever received graciously.

"A complete and utter failure? Look, just because I got a divorce doesn't mean I'm a failure. I run one of the biggest ranches in Texas and run it damn well."

Her eyes widened, and she shook her head. "Oh, no. I wasn't talking about you being a failure, Rome. I was talking about me."

Before he could ask her what she meant, Liberty came charging around the corner of the barn. While Cloe was calm, soft spoken, and blended into the woodwork, Liberty was high strung, controlling, and commanded attention with her stunning beauty. At one time, Rome had considered asking her out, but she scared him too much.

"Have you seen Sweetie and Decker? We're getting ready to take pictures and I can't find them anywhere. I swear trying to keep control of a bridal party after the wedding is over is like trying to corral a litter of misbehaving puppies." Liberty glanced between Cloe and Rome. "Just what are you two doing hiding over here? And why are you holding Rome's hat, Cloe?"

Rome waited for Cloe to tell her sister about his panic attack.

She didn't.

"I was feeling a little lightheaded from the heat in the barn and Rome helped me outside to get some fresh air." She fanned herself with his hat, causing the wisps of hair around her face to flutter. What *was* her hair color? Mahogany?

"Lightheaded?" Liberty said. "You've never been lightheaded in your life, Clo—" She cut off and her eyes widened. "Wait a second. Are you pregnant? Is that why Brandon has finally gotten around to asking you to marry him after six long years?"

Rome glanced at Cloe, whose face was as red

as the barn. She was getting married? Why did that surprise him? Probably because she had never dated in high school or even shown any interest in dating. Which had made him assume she would end up like his Aunt Francis, who was quite happy living alone in South Padre with her three parakeets.

"I'm not pregnant," Cloe said.

Liberty's eyes narrowed. "Then why were you lightheaded? And don't give me that ridiculous excuse about the barn being hot. It's not over sixty degrees today."

Since Cloe had lied for him, Rome jumped in and helped her out. "I guess some people are just more hot natured than others. I was burning up in the barn."

Liberty studied him. "You do look sweaty. You might want to wipe some of that off before pictures." She glanced at Cloe. "And take off that ugly scarf, Clo. No wonder you're overheated with that thing wrapped around your neck." She reached for the scarf, but Cloe sent her a warning look.

"The scarf stays, Libby."

Rome was surprised. He'd always viewed Cloe as a wilting pansy next to her more aggressive sisters. But it looked like she had some steel hidden under her quiet reserve.

Liberty backed off. "Fine. Keep the scarf, but you two don't dawdle. Since I can't find Decker and Sweetie, we'll start on the groomsmen's and bridesmaids' photos." She whirled and hurried off as quickly as she had arrived.

"I see Liberty is still a tornado." Rome took his hat from Cloe and pulled it on. "So you're getting married. Congratulations."

Instead of replying, she studied him for a long moment before she stepped closer and reached up to adjust his hat. He didn't know what surprised him most. Her uncharacteristic actions, or the realization that he'd been wrong about her eyes. They weren't the same color as her sisters'. This close, he could see that the irises were a darker shade of green. Like the color of the late summer grass that covered the south pasture.

And how did she know how he liked his hat to sit?

She adjusted it to the perfect angle on his head as she spoke. "Actually, I'm not getting married. Brandon broke up with me a few weeks ago. I just haven't gotten around to telling my family yet. I didn't want to ruin Sweetie's wedding with bad news."

Rome felt like a complete jerk. While Cloe had been trying to make him feel better about having a panic attack, she had been suffering from her own relationship ending only weeks ago. A six-year relationship.

"I'm sorry," he said.

She brushed something off the brim of his hat before she stepped back. "It's okay. Technically, we weren't even engaged. I only thought he was going to ask me to marry him . . . instead, he told me he didn't think we were well suited for each other and asked if I would consider trans ferring to another school so things wouldn't be awkward."

"Another school?"

She nodded. "He and I work at the same elementary school in College Station."

Rome snorted. "I hope you told him go to hell."

"Why would I do that? He was right. It would be awkward seeing him at school every day."

Rome was struck speechless. Most women he knew would have set the guy's desk on fire . . . after tying him to it. Emily had had a raging screaming fit when Rome had forgotten their three-month dating anniversary. Which should have been an indication of her temper tantrums to come. Now that he thought about it, he had never heard Cloe even raise her voice. She had always been calm and rational.

"It worked out for the best," she continued. "I wanted to take an extended leave of absence anyway so I could help get the ranch ready to sell."

Rome knew the Holiday Ranch was in financial trouble. People who had owned their land as long as the Holidays didn't sell unless they had to. It was too bad. He never liked to see a ranch go under.

"So when does your ranch go on the market?" he asked.

"Probably after the wedding. You think your daddy would be interested in buying it?"

Rome laughed. "You and I both know that your daddy doesn't want my daddy owning any part of his ranch. And my daddy would never act like he was interested in Holiday land . . . even if buying it was the smart thing to do."

Cloe's summer-grass green eyes grew intense. "If you feel that way, then why don't you buy it?"

Before Rome could get over his surprise at the question, Liberty came charging around the corner of the barn again. "I swear I'm going to start thinking there's something going on between you two if you don't stop hiding behind this barn. Now, come on. It's picture time!"

Rome followed behind the two Holiday sisters with his mind still trying to absorb Cloe's question.

Him? Buy the Holiday Ranch?

It was a foolish notion. His father would have a fit if Rome made an offer on his archenemy's ranch. And Hank Holiday would never accept an offer from a Remington . . . unless the Holidays' financial problems were worse than Rome thought. Why else would Cloe have posed the question?

If that were the case, then maybe the Remington-Holiday feud was about to come to an end.

CHAPTER TWO

CLOE HATED TO be photographed. She either smiled so big she looked like the Joker or she smiled too little and looked like she was constipated. It didn't help that the updo Belle had put her hair in kept sliding farther and farther to the side of her head. Or the scarf she wore really *was* ugly.

But she wasn't about to take it off.

She had asked Liberty to order her a conservative dress. She should have known her anything-but-conservative sister would do just the opposite and order one that was too short with a plunging neckline. Cloe had been able to let down the hem, but her sewing skills weren't good enough to fix a neckline and she'd hated to ask her mama when her mama had been busy getting ready for the wedding. So Cloe had improvised with a scarf.

Over the years, she had become an expert at disguising her overly large breasts with scarfs and loose clothing. For a person who didn't like to attract attention to herself, big boobs were the bane of her existence.

"How you holdin' up?"

Rome's whispered question pulled her out of her thoughts. She wanted to turn and look at him, but she didn't dare when Liberty had just finished posing them. Rome stood close behind her with his hands on her waist and his heat radiating around her like an electric blanket, making her feel completely flustered.

Which was why she had always steered clear of the oldest Remington. There was something about Rome that unnerved her. It wasn't because of anything he did. He'd always been pleasant and polite. It was more a physical reaction she couldn't quite put her finger on. It took a real effort to ignore the jumpy feeling in her stomach and answer him.

"I'm f-f-fine."

"If you're fine, why are you so tense?" His hands tightened, his fingers brushing her hipbones and sending a tingle running through her from the top of her head to the tips of her toes. She sucked in a startled breath and her nose filled with a scent that was soothing and confusingly familiar. While she was trying to figure out where she had smelled the scent before, he spoke again.

"I was just thinking. What if, for one night, we forget about our past relationships and enjoy the reception . . . together."

She completely forgot about keeping her pose and turned to him. "Together?"

His eyes twinkled. They were the most unusual shade. Not quite blue but not quite gray. Like mist on a mountain lake. "Why not? You don't have a date and I don't have a date. It could be fun."

Fun? No one had ever looked to Cloe for fun. She wasn't the type of person who threw caution to the wind and had a night of frivolous fun. She wasn't frivolous. And she certainly wasn't fun. She was logical. And her logical brain told her that the only reason Rome was asking her to be his date was because she had helped him through a panic attack and he felt like he owed her.

Rome had never liked owing people. When he forgot his lunch in first grade and she'd shared her peanut-butter-and-banana sandwich with him, the next day, she found a sack lunch in her backpack with a peanut-butter-and-banana sandwich, Cheetos, and a Snickers candy bar. When she had loaned him a pencil in third grade, the next day, he had brought her an entire pack of pencils. It was just the way Rome was. He believed in paying his debts in full.

But she wasn't a debt.

"You don't owe me anything, Rome," she said. "I was happy to help."

He squinted at her. "I didn't ask you because I thought I owed you. I asked you because I thought it might make us both feel better."

Cloe wished it was that simple. But spending the evening with a handsome cowboy wasn't going to make her feel better. Not when all her plans for the future had come crumbling down around her.

She had been so certain she and Brandon were the perfect match. He was as logical and organized as she was. He kept his well-thought-out schedule on his phone calendar and was never late to anything. He didn't drink or dance and enjoyed quiet nights at home. And he loved children and teaching as much as she did.

That was how they met. They both attended Texas A&M. They kept bumping into each other around campus and finally Brandon had asked her out. They had dated all through college and then had gotten jobs at the same elementary school—him as a fifth grade teacher and her as a speech pathologist.

A year later, Brandon had asked her to move in with him. She'd just assumed marriage was the next step. She wasn't even concerned when three years passed without one mention of marriage. Like her, Brandon liked to take his time whenever he made a big decision. When he had told her they needed to have a serious talk about their relationship, she just knew he was finally going to pop the question.

Instead, he had popped her heart.

"So what do you say?"

Rome's question pulled her from her thoughts and she answered it honestly. "Thank you for the offer, Rome, but you don't want to be stuck with me all night when there is an entire barn filled with single women who would love to make you feel better."

"Just so you know, I wouldn't consider an evening spent with you as being stuck. In fact, it's just the opposite. If I go in the barn without a date, I'll be stuck asking every single female at the reception to dance. While I don't mind shuffling through a slow waltz with Mrs. Stokes, I flat out refuse to dance with Pippin Wadley again. Last time I let that little four-year-old hellion climb up on my boots so I could teach her the two-step, she bit my leg because I wasn't moving fast enough."

Even though her heart was heavy, she couldn't help laughing at the image of a little girl standing on Rome's boots and sinking her teeth into his leg as he two-stepped her around the dance floor.

His gray eyes narrowed beneath the brim of his Stetson. "Wait a second. Was that a laugh?" He grinned. "See, we *can* make each other feel better."

Thankfully, before Cloe had to decline Rome again, Sweetie and Decker finally showed up. From the looks of their disheveled hair and clothes, it was obvious what they'd been doing. When Sweetie moved next to her for group pictures, Cloe, discreetly, buttoned a button on the back of Sweetie's wedding gown and plucked a few pieces of hay from her hair.

After the group pictures were finished, Cloe posed with her sisters. She knew all five of her sisters were thinking the same thing she was: these could be the last pictures they ever took together at the ranch. The last time they were photographed with the huge red barn looming behind them. Or crowded together on the front porch steps of their two-story farmhouse. Or standing beneath the big oak with the rope swing.

It took a real effort to smile.

Holiday Ranch had been in their family for over a century. It had never been a huge cattle ranch like the Remingtons', but it had been big enough to support their family and give Cloe and her sisters a wonderful childhood of riding horses, swimming in the springs, sleeping in the hayloft, and enjoying every acre of land that had been passed down over generations.

Unfortunately, low cattle prices and her father's greed for more land had led to a growing debt that only selling the ranch would fix. Cloe had hoped they could hang on to the acre of land with the house and barn, but she'd just learned from the Realtor that the chances of selling the land for the money they needed without the house and barn were slim to none.

Of course, selling wasn't even the main problem. The main problem was her grandmother. Mimi's name was on the title of the ranch and she had no intentions of selling her home. Instead she had come up with a crazy scheme to keep the ranch in the family by marrying one of her granddaughters off to a wealthy Remington. As soon as she, Mama, and Daddy joined them for a family photo, Mimi started in.

"Did you notice how cute Noelle and Casey Remington looked coming down the aisle together?" Mimi's voice rose from beneath the wide brim of one of the many gardening hats she loved to wear.

"Cute?" Noelle kept smiling for the camera and spoke through her teeth. "Casey and I are about as cute as a baby lamb in a tiger's mouth,

Mimi. That man is the bane of my existence. So don't even think I'm going to be part of your crazy plan to save the ranch by sacrificing one of us to a Remington."

"Both of you lower your voices," Mama scolded with a smile pinned on her face. "The Remingtons are standing right over there."

Casey and Rome stood by the barn talking. Most people thought Casey was the most handsome Remington with his perfect features, golden hair, and charming smile. Rome's features weren't perfect. His nose was prominent and had a bump on the bridge from being hit with a stall door when he was a kid. His hair was jet black like his father's and had a tendency to curl when it rained. His smile wasn't charming, In fact, he didn't smile nearly as often as his brother. And when he did, it was more hesitate and subdued.

Of course, Cloe now understood why.

She had heard gossip about his wife leaving him. The townsfolk thought he was well over it. Today proved otherwise. She could sympathize with him. It was difficult being the one who was left. It made you feel defective. Like a broken toy returned to the store. After six years, she couldn't stop wondering why Brandon had decided she wasn't worth keeping.

As soon as the photographer was finished, Liberty lined them up in the order she wanted them to enter the barn for the reception. Once again, Cloe was paired up with Rome. When they reached the table set up for the wedding party, he pulled out a chair for her and winked.

"It looks like we're stuck together whether you want to be or not."

Thankfully, Cloe's little sister, Hallie, took a seat on the other side of him. Unlike Cloe, Hallie had always been a talker. All through dinner, she kept Rome in a lively conversation about ranching, football, and beer brewing while Cloe tried not to worry about her upcoming maid-of-honor toast.

As a childhood stutterer, speaking in front of large crowds had always been a terrifying experience for her. Whenever she had to make a speech, she spent countless hours practicing what she would say in front of a mirror. She'd done the same thing for her toast, but she still pulled out her cellphone and opened her notes so she could go over it.

She was feeling pretty confident until Belle brought her the microphone and Cloe stood and looked into her big sister's beloved green eyes. Then all her emotions welled to the surface and the toast she had painstakingly memorized got all scrambled up in her head.

As she stood there struggling to remember her speech, people started glancing at each other. Before she could completely embarrass herself, her cellphone was pressed into her hand. With flaming cheeks, she lifted her phone and read her toast in a robotic voice. Once she'd finished, she quickly handed the microphone to Rome and took her seat.

Of course, Rome didn't need notes to help him. Nor did he sound like a robot when he spoke.

"I always thought Decker wasn't the marrying kind. He didn't date much and rarely wanted to go to the Hellhole for a beer. He seemed content to spend his time protecting this town and hanging out with his hound dog, George Strait. But then, Sweetie Holiday came back to town and my laid-back best friend wasn't so laid back anymore. In fact, he became downright ornery." Everyone laughed and nodded their heads in agreement. "I realized I was wrong. Decker *was* the marrying kind. He had just been patiently waiting for the right woman. When that right woman showed up, he didn't waste any time getting down on one knee."

The right woman.

The words rang through Cloe's head like the First Baptist Church bell on Sunday morning. They were the exact words Brandon had used when he'd broken up with her. *I don't think you're the right woman for me.* All the emotions Cloe had been keeping at bay since the breakup slammed into her like a runaway semi truck.

She now knew exactly how Rome had felt earlier. She was about to have a panic attack . . . or start bawling like a baby. After her embarrassing toast, she wasn't about to let that happen in front of the entire town. As soon as Rome finished his toast, she quickly slipped out of her chair.

She wanted to head back to the house and curl up on her childhood bed until morning. But in order to get out of the barn, she would have to wind her way through the tables filled with partying townsfolk and someone was bound to stop her. She couldn't talk to anyone right now without breaking down.

Frantic to escape, she glanced around. The ladder to the hayloft caught her attention. The hayloft had always been a place of sanctuary for the Holiday sisters. A place they congregated together or went to alone when they needed a moment to themselves.

And if anyone needed a moment to herself, it was Cloe.

While everyone watched Sweetie and Decker dance their first dance, Cloe quickly climbed the ladder. Once in the loft, she discovered where Sweetie and Decker had been hiding. The satiny comforter thrown over the mound of fresh straw still held the indentation of two bodies. A bottle of opened champagne sat in a bucket of ice, two fluted glasses sitting next to it.

It was a perfect love nest.

Anger welled up inside of Cloe. Not at Sweetie—she wanted nothing but happiness for her sister—but at the injustice of it all. Until a few weeks ago, Cloe had been the only one who had a steady boyfriend. The only one who had wanted to get married and start a family. And now Sweetie was happily married and Cloe was standing in her sister's love nest feeling like a pathetic fool.

Of course, it made sense. Sweetie was beautiful and charming and talented. All of Cloe's sisters were. Cloe was the oddball of the family. The stutterer who didn't talk in front of anyone but her family until she was almost ten. The Plain

Jane who faded into the background. The average sister who never excelled at anything. She had been a good student but not an excellent one. A good horsewoman but no better than any other ranch kid. A softball player who spent most of her time warming the bench. A church choir member who never got asked to sing a solo.

No wonder Brandon hadn't wanted her.

Who in their right mind would?

She was the invisible woman.

There, but not seen.

CHAPTER THREE

A S CLOE'S YOUNGER sister, Hallie, talked on and on about how to make the best beer, Rome's mind returned to the six words that had been swirling around in his head ever since Cloe had spoken them.

Then why don't you buy it?

He had convinced himself there was no way he could get his hands on the ranch. Now he was wondering if there was a chance Hank would sell him the ranch. Why else would Cloe offer him the opportunity?

Just the thought of owning the ranch made Rome feel giddy. While it wasn't as big as the Remington Ranch, Hank owned a prime piece of cattle land with a spring fed by a below-ground aquifer. The state of Texas owned all surface water like rivers and lakes, but ground water belonged to the owner of the property. For a cattleman, having your own water source was like having your own gold mine.

And it wasn't just the springs. He glanced out the open door to the two-story farmhouse. If he bought the Holiday Ranch, he wouldn't have to live under his father's roof anymore. He'd have his own place. His own barn. His own land.

Of course, his father wouldn't be happy about it. Sam liked having Rome under his thumb. He also wouldn't want Hank thinking that a Remington coveted anything of the Holidays'. But the more Rome thought about owning his own plot of land, the more he coveted the Holiday Ranch.

"Have you seen Cloe, Hallie?"

The question pulled Rome from his thoughts and he glanced over to see Belle Holiday standing there. Belle was Liberty's twin sister. They looked exactly alike, but were easy to tell apart as soon as they opened their mouths. Belle was soft spoken and reserved.

"Liberty said Cloe was feeling lightheaded earlier and I'm worried because I can't seem to find her anywhere."

"Lightheaded?" Hallie scoffed. "That doesn't sound like our sister. Cloe has never been lightheaded in her life. If anything, her brain is too heavy. She won't make a single decision without overthinking it."

Belle smiled at Hallie. "Unlike some people, who jump without looking?"

"I look. I just don't hesitate."

Rome laughed. Hallie had always had a sassy personality and jumped into things without too much thought. Rome was more like Cloe. He thought things through from all angles before making a decision.

Buying the Holiday Ranch was a good decision.

Since Cloe seemed to be helping her parents sell the ranch, it wouldn't hurt to get her on his side.

He got up. "I'll help you look for Cloe. Y'all check out the reception and I'll check outside. Maybe she just needed a breath of fresh air."

But making his way outside wasn't easy. If the men didn't stop him to talk about ranching, trucks, and the Wilder Wildcats' chances of winning another high school state football championship, the women stopped him to ask why he hadn't brought a date and if his daddy was ticked off about Rome attending the wedding at the Holiday Ranch.

Sam hadn't said a word about Rome coming to the wedding and being Decker's best man. His father had always chosen his battles. Rome figured wanting to buy the Holiday Ranch was going to be one battle Sam chose.

After Rome finally made his way outside, he headed around to the side of the barn where Cloe had taken him earlier. He stopped in his tracks when he saw the glow of a lit cigarette. But before he could turn right back around and escape, Fiona Stokes spoke.

"Where you running off to, Rome Remington?"

Rome mentally groaned before he plastered on a smile and moved closer. Mrs. Stokes leaned against the side of the barn like an old hooker on a street corner. The ratty mink stole she always wore encircled her frail shoulders and the lit cig arette hung from her bottom lip as if superglued there as a circle of smoke enshrouded her head.

"Evenin', Ms. Stokes." He tipped his hat. "How are you enjoying the reception?"

"I've been to better. My third marriage was a humdinger of a party. Folks didn't leave until close to two in the morning. Of course, Buford and I continued the party in our hotel suite until dawn. We tore that room up like a rock band high on cocaine."

Rome cringed. The last thing he wanted to hear about was Mrs. Stokes's sex life. He was relieved when she changed the subject.

"So are you out here hiding from all those single ladies hoping to snag themselves a wealthy rancher? Everyone in Wilder knows your daddy wants you to get married again and give him some grandbabies. Hopefully, your next marriage will go better than your last one. Anyone with eyes could see that bit of fluff you brought home from college didn't belong on a ranch."

This was the reason Rome hated living in a small town. Nothing was personal and private. He tried to keep his smile in place. "Actually, I'm not wife-hunting tonight. I'm looking for Cloe Holiday. Her sisters are worried about her."

Mrs. Stokes took a long drag of her cigarette before she spoke in a release of smoke. "There's no need to worry about that one. She's always had a good head on her shoulders. And she didn't leave. I saw her go up to the hayloft."

The hayloft? Why had she gone up there?

"Thanks, Ms—"

Mrs. Stokes started coughing. Everyone in town knew you didn't leave during Mrs. Stokes's coughing fits. It pissed her off. So Rome had to politely wait. As always, she started talking as soon as the last cough was over.

"I heard she was gettin' married to some man from College Station." She shook her head. "A shame. I was hopin' she'd come back home to live now that Sweetie has."

He didn't want to give away Cloe's secret, but he also had lived through the townsfolk gossiping about him being the cause of his wife running off. He didn't want Cloe going through the same thing.

"Maybe she will move home," he said. "I heard she decided she wasn't ready to get married and broke things off. I guess the guy was an idiot."

Her eyes narrowed on him as she took another drag of her cigarette. "Is that so? Well, like I said, that girl has a good head on her shoulders."

He nodded. "Always has. Now I better get back to looking for her."

A smile tipped Mrs. Stokes's wrinkled lips. "I'm sure you'll find her. You've always been a determined boy."

Rome tipped his hat before he headed back inside.

A line dance had started and most of the townsfolk were on the dance floor and too busy to stop Rome as he made his way to the hayloft ladder at the back of the barn. He wasn't sure what he'd find when he reached the top, but it wasn't a scene for seduction.

Battery-powered camp lanterns filled the loft with a soft hazy glow. In front of the open hay doors, a puffy comforter had been spread over a fresh pile of straw. Next to it was a champagne bucket filled with ice and two fluted glasses.

So this was why Cloe had declined his offer to be his date. She had other plans. No wonder she hadn't acted all that upset over her breakup. Obviously, she had another man waiting in the wings. He shook his head. It was always the quiet ones that surprised you. He started to move back down the ladder when a voice stopped him.

"'Romeo, Romeo, wherefore art thou, Romeo?'"

He squinted at the dark corner where the voice had come from. "Cloe?"

She stepped out of the shadows. The tower of hair had fallen and a mass of reddish-brown curls surrounded her face and fell around her shoulders. Her glasses were gone and so were her boots. She swayed on bare feet littered with straw. In her hand was the champagne bottle that had been missing from the bucket.

She waved it around. "Yes, it's me. Invisible Cloe Holiday."

Rome glanced back at the shadows. "Are you alone?"

"Why, yes I am. Completely and utterly alone. And you know what? I'm probably gonna die alone. Because I'm not the right woman. I'm the wrong woman. All wrong." She lifted the champagne bottle to her lips and tipped it. But it looked like she had already drained it dry. She lowered the bottle and sighed. "Well, shit."

Rome didn't know what surprised him most—the cussing or the drinking. Both were completely out of character for Cloe. At least, she hadn't used to cuss and drink . . . or plan sexual rendezvouses with men.

Maybe this had more to do with the breakup. He knew for a fact that getting your heart broken could make you act out of character. He had gotten drunk and hooked up with a number of random women after Emily had left him. He was lucky nothing bad had come from it. Randomly hooking up right after your heart got broken wasn't a good idea. Especially when alcohol was involved. And while Rome trusted most of the men in town to act like gentlemen with an inebriated woman, there were a few men he didn't trust as far as he could throw them. Like Cob Ritter. Cob had somehow finagled an invitation to the wedding. No doubt as someone's plus one. The thought of him taking advantage of Cloe didn't sit well with Rome.

"Who are you waiting for?" he asked.

"My Romeo, of course. Isn't that who all girls are waiting for? The one man who can't live without them and is willing to scale garden walls and recite sonnets and go against their entire family just for a chance to let lips do what hands do."

Rome squinted. Where was the levelheaded, practical girl he'd been talking to earlier?

"So who is this Romeo?"

She tossed the empty bottle at the ice bucket. It

missed and rolled across the floor. "Well, it wasn't Brandon. Now was it?" She wobbled her head from side to side. "Nope. I waited around for him to pop the question and all he popped was my heart with all the reasons I'm not the woman for him. And maybe waiting around was my problem. Maybe I should do what my sister Hallie does and just take the horns by the bull." She gave him a thorough once-over. "Do you have a horn, bull?"

He couldn't help grinning. This side of Cloe was unexpected . . . and intriguing. "I do, but I don't think I can let you take a hold of it when you're as drunk as Cooter Brown."

"Who is Cooter Brown, anyway? And why has the poor man become synonymous with intoxicated people? What if he had a broken heart and was just drowning his sorrows? And now the entire world thinks of him as a perfect analogy for a drunk."

He should have known Cloe would be an intelligent drunk. "Okay. Why don't you sit right down there on that blanket and I'll go get you some water?"

"I don't want water. I want . . . a margarita! I've never had one and now I want one. And you know why I never had one?" She didn't wait for a reply. "Because I'm always the designated driver. It's my job to watch out for my sisters. To make sure they have a good time, but don't drive drunk. But you know what? Maybe it's time I have a good time. Maybe it's time I drink and dance and have fun." She awkwardly twirled around before she stumbled to a stop and fanned herself with a hand. "Is it hot in here? Because I feel extremely hot." She tugged at her scarf, but all she succeeded in doing was pulling it tighter around her throat.

Worried she was going to choke herself, Rome walked over to help. But the way she had attached it wasn't easy to figure out. He finally located a small knot at the back of her neck. He turned her away from him and pushed the pile of curls out of the way. It was hard not to notice the way the silky strands slid through his fingers as he shifted the mass of hair over her shoulder.

It wasn't just a dull reddish-brown. It was a wealth of auburn curls that reflected the lanterns' glow like a bushel of shiny burgundy apples.

Why would she hide such glorious hair in ties and clips?

The knot was tight and it took him a while to loose it. She stood perfectly still with her head bowed. After a long moment, she spoke in a soft whisper that he had to strain to hear.

"You know what else is hot? You. Your touch makes me feel . . . scorched."

His fingers stilled at the nape of her neck. Her skin was as soft as a baby chick's downy feathers and he wanted nothing more than to run his fingers over it. Instead, he pushed the thought away and concentrated on not touching her as he continued to work on the knot.

And she continued to talk.

"I've never felt burned by a man before . . . not even Brandon. He wasn't hot. He was lukewarm at best. Brushes of his fingers never made my tummy tingle or my insides feel like they're melting."

Talk about hot. Rome suddenly felt like the loft had turned into a furnace. One he needed to get out of before he did something he would regret later. Hank would never sell him the ranch if he seduced his daughter.

He heaved a sigh of relief when the knot came undone. His relief was short lived when he pulled the scarf free and Cloe turned around. Her hair wasn't the only thing she'd been hiding. Above the low neckline of the dress, mouthwatering breasts swelled like two pale loaves of rising bread.

Rome was dumbstruck.

Cloe Holiday was stacked. Like jaw-dropping, brick-shithouse stacked. And Rome didn't know if he was more stunned by the fact she had big boobs or the fact he had never noticed.

"Holy shit." He hadn't meant to speak the words aloud, but . . . *Holy Shit*.

Cloe placed a hand over her swelling cleavage and looked stricken. "I know. They're too big. All my sisters got medium-sized or little boobs and I got these."

He shook his head. "No, I didn't mean holy shit in a bad way."

She looked confused. "Then what way did you mean it?"

Realizing there was no way to explain it without coming off as a boob-crazy jerk, he shrugged. "I was just surprised. I didn't realize you were so . . ." He struggled to find the right word. Cloe helped him out.

"Huge. Gigantic. Obscenely mammoth."

He sighed, knowing he was just going to have to come off as a jerk. "None of the above. While you might think they're too big, most men would agree that there's no such thing as too big when it comes to women's breasts."

She lowered her hand. "So you like them?"

He glanced down. Like was too mild a word for what he felt about the bountiful beauty before him. He cleared his throat. "Umm . . . well, yes. They're nice."

She frowned. "Nice?"

He decided it would be best to leave things right where they were. "I'm going to go get you that bottle of water. If you tell me the name of the guy you were meeting, I'll let him know you've had a little too much champagne and he'll have to take a rain check."

"The guy I'm meeting?"

He glanced around. "The guy you set all this up for."

A big smile lit her face before she started to laugh. He'd never seen her out-and-out laugh with her head tipped back and her eyes twinkling and two cute little dimples winking. As he watched her, a strange feeling settled in his stomach. A feeling that only could be described as a . . . tummy tingle. He shook his head and turned for the ladder.

As he was grabbing a couple bottles of water

from a cooler by the refreshment table, he ran into Belle.

"Cloe's fine," he said. "She's in the hayloft." He left out the part about the seductive scene and her inebriated state. He figured Cloe wouldn't want her family to know about either. "I think she just needed a break."

Belle smiled. "That sounds like Cloe. She never has enjoyed big parties." A commotion broke out on the other side of the barn and she shook her head as she hurried off. "I wish I could hide in the hayloft."

When Rome got to the top of the ladder, he discovered the lanterns had been turned off. The only light came from the moonlight shining in the open hay hatch doors.

"Cloe?"

His only answer was a gentle snoring. He followed the sound and found her wrapped in the comforter like a burrito with only the top of her head peeking out. He couldn't help but smile at the sight.

He should leave. It looked like the guy she had planned to meet had stood her up and he figured Belle would be checking on her soon enough. But for some reason—probably because he didn't like big parties either—he didn't leave. Instead, he set down the water bottles, took off his hat and his jacket, and moved to the open hatch door.

The Holidays' big farmhouse stood only yards away from the barn, its windows warmly lit and its front door decorated with a heart wreath. With its huge porch and blooming flower gardens, it looked like it belonged in a country home and garden magazine. Rome wouldn't be surprised to hear John-Boy's voice ringing out, wishing his family a good night.

In comparison, the Remington's house was cold and sterile. Of course, it had never known a woman's touch. His mama, Glorieta Remington, had left when Rome was only four. So if she had left her touch, it was long gone by the time Rome had gotten old enough to notice. And Emily had never taken the time to make the house her own. It was like she had known her marriage to Rome wasn't going to last.

If he had owned his own place, would Emily have left? It couldn't have been easy to live with three arrogant men. Emily had never gotten along with his father or brother. Rome could understand not getting along with Sam. Few people could. But everyone got along with Casey. And maybe they would have gotten along if they hadn't had to live together. Maybe things would have been different if Emily had had her own home.

Although she still would have been on a ranch. It was the isolation she'd hated the most.

Something Rome loved.

He pulled his attention from the house and looked at the wide expanse of land behind it.

He loved looking out on miles and miles of grazing land without one house or building to take away from its natural beauty. What would it feel like if all this land belonged to him? Land that he could do with what he wanted without running anything by his father? Sam was a smart businessman, but some of his beliefs were antiquated and he had no desire to change them. He refused to even consider new ranching techniques. But if Rome owned his own ranch, he could try solar-powered property monitoring and precision agriculture. He could move out from under the shadow of his father and prove himself.

A soft snoring pulled him from his thoughts and he turned away from the open hatch door and looked at Cloe. She had pushed down the comforter and moonlight fell over her face turning her skin to creamy buttermilk. Long lashes rested against high cheekbones that were flushed a soft pink. Her button nose boasted a sprinkling of freckles. Her lips weren't full, but they weren't thin either. They had a cute bow with just enough plump to make him wonder how they would feel pressed against his.

People had always referred to Cloe as the Plain Jane of the Holiday sisters. Rome hadn't joined in on the gossip, but he'd silently agreed. Now he realized they'd all been wrong. While she wasn't as gorgeous as Liberty or Belle, or as cute as Noelle and Hallie, or as pretty as Sweetie, Cloe had an understated beauty. A beauty that snuck up on you. Like the soft pink of dawn long before the sun peeks its head above the horizon. Or the calm stillness of a lake on a windless day. Or crystal snowflakes drifting down from a dark night sky.

Her beauty was understated and peaceful.

Rome couldn't remember the last time he'd felt peaceful.

CHAPTER FOUR

CLOE WOKE TO a throbbing headache, a queasy stomach . . . and the feeling of being tucked inside a warm cocoon. She cracked open her eyes, then slammed them shut again when brilliant rays of sunshine sliced through her retinas like her mama's serrated kitchen knife slicing through August-ripened tomatoes. She groaned and snuggled deeper into the cocoon that surrounded her, wiggling her bottom until it was perfectly nestled in the cave of heat.

A cave that had a snake in it.

Beneath her butt cheeks she could feel its hard length twitch as if waking up.

Her eyes flashed open and she ignored the pain of the bright sunlight as she tried to figure out where she was. The smell of hay and the weathered pine walls gave her the answer.

She must have fallen asleep in the hayloft after her major meltdown. Thankfully, no one had witnessed it . . . no one but her Romeo.

She squeezed her eyes shut as memories flooded back of everything she'd said to Rome when she'd been drunk on champagne. How would she ever face the man again? And maybe she wouldn't have to. If she stayed away from town and kept to the ranch, she might be able to avoid him until she left town to head back to College Station.

A throat clearing right next to her ear had her almost jumping out of her skin.

"Do you think you could let go of my arm?"

She glanced down and saw her arm resting on a dark-haired, muscled forearm in a cuffed white tuxedo shirt. Her hand was cradling the large hand attached to that arm, pressing it against her breasts.

"Oh my God!" She shoved the arm away before scrambling off the comforter and jumping to her feet.

The sight that greeted her left her completely at a loss for words.

Rome Remington was stretched out on the pile of hay with his black hair mussed and his tuxedo shirt unbuttoned, revealing a muscled chest with a thatch of dark hair narrowing to a skinny line that trailed all the way down to the waistband of pants.

Pants that sported a lengthy . . . snake.

Cloe's eyes widened as she realized what she had been cuddled up to. Her face flamed.

So did her entire body.

Rome didn't seem to be aware of her embarrassment. He squinted in the bright sunlight streaming in through the open hay doors of the loft for a long moment before he sat up and stretched his hands over his head and yawned.

Her great-grandmothers could have scrubbed clothes on his washboard stomach.

"Good mornin'."

All Cloe could do was stare. How could he look so gorgeous after spending the night in a pile of hay? She probably looked like she'd been living in a chicken coop for a month. She tried to smooth her hair and came away with a handful of straw, confirming her suspicions.

He leaned over and grabbed one of the bottles of water sitting on the floor and held it out. "Here. It helps to stay hydrated."

She didn't take the bottle. Her mind was too consumed with something else. "We didn't . . ." She struggled to find the right word and came up empty. "Did we?"

He effortlessly rolled to his feet. "No, we didn't. I don't take advantage of inebriated women." A smile tipped his lips as his gaze ran over her. His eyes twinkled when they lifted. "Now if you'd been sober, it might have been a different story."

She blinked at him, and then realized he was only kidding. There was no way Rome Remington would make a pass at her. She laughed. "Well, thank you for being so honorable."

"That's me. Honorable to a fault." He held out the bottle of water. "So how are you feeling this morning?"

She started to say fine, but then told the truth. "Horrible."

"Physically or emotionally?"

She took the bottle of water and opened it. "Both. Using champagne to drown my sorrows was one of the stupidest things I've ever done. I'm sorry you had to witness it."

"It wasn't a big deal. Believe me, I did plenty of drowning when Emily left me."

She lowered the bottle she'd just taken a sip from. "Did it help?"

He sighed. "Not at all. But you'll try just about anything to take away the sting of rejection." He sat down on a hay bale and started pulling on his boots. "Now I better get going. Daddy doesn't mind me and Casey staying out all night as long as we're home bright and early to get our work done."

At the mention of his family, her eyes widened. "Oh, no! My family must be worried sick." She frantically started searching for her socks and boots. Rome stopped her.

"Relax. I told Belle you were hiding out in the hayloft."

That explained why her sisters and her parents hadn't come looking for her. This wasn't the first time Cloe or one of her sisters had spent the night in the hayloft. In a large family filled with stubborn, opinionated people, the hayloft had become a sanctuary the sisters all fought over. Last night, Cloe had needed a sanctuary. She just hadn't planned on sharing it with the man looking back at her with misty gray eyes.

"I wasn't hiding," she said.

"No, you were just waiting for your Romeo. Who is he?"

She blushed as she turned away and continued

to look for her socks and boots. "I was drunk and rambling. There was no Romeo."

"Then why the comforter, lanterns, and champagne? It didn't look like you were waiting for your grandma."

She found her boots and socks and sat down on a bale of hay across from him to put them on. "The loft was like this when I got here. Decker or Sweetie must have set everything up."

"That explains why they were late for pictures." He chuckled as he finished tugging on his boots. "I guess you didn't need a bodyguard after all."

"A bodyguard?"

"I don't seduce inebriated women and I don't want any one else doing it either."

All Cloe could do was stare at him in disbelief. He had stayed the night with her to protect her honor?

He must have read her thoughts because he shrugged. "Like I said, honorable to a fault." He got to his feet and then held out his hand to help her to hers. She didn't know where he'd found them, but suddenly he was slipping her glasses on and gently pushing them up the bridge of her nose.

"There," he said. "Better?"

She *could* see better. Which wasn't a good thing. Rome was standing much too close. The bright morning sun was behind him, casting a heavenly aura that made his hair look almost blue and his eyes look even grayer. They had always been intense. Rome was an intense man. But that intensity had never been focused on Cloe like it was now.

"So you don't want a man climbing to your balcony and speaking of his undying love?" he asked.

She shook her head. "I would be worried the entire time that he'd slip and fall to his death."

Rome laughed. "So no balcony climbing. What about poetry?"

"I don't need fancy words." She hesitated as thoughts of Brandon filtered into her mind. "But maybe that was my problem. I never expected Brandon to write sonnets about his undying love or send me roses or take me on special dates. Maybe if I had, he'd have valued me more."

Once the words were out, she felt foolish. She had no business sharing such personal thoughts with Rome. She started to apologize, but he spoke before she could.

"I thought the same thing when Emily left. I thought if I had just done things differently, she would have stayed. But that's the funny thing about the past, you can't go back and fix it. No matter how much you might want to."

She shook her head sadly. "No, you can't." A strand of hair fell over her eye, but before she could push it back, Rome did, his hot fingers streaking her cheek with fire as he tucked it behind her ear. His hand remained there. His eyes intense as they looked into hers.

"Then I guess all we can do is move forward."

For a second, she thought he was going to kiss her. He shifted closer, his head drifting to one side as his lips parted. But before those lips could touch hers, a humming drifted in through the open doors of the loft and whatever spell that had been cast was broken.

Her eyes widened. "Mimi!" Without hesitation, she grabbed the front of his tuxedo shirt and pulled him toward the ladder. Or tried to. It was like trying to move a brick wall. "You need to get out of here and you need to get out of here now." If Mimi caught them together, she would think Cloe had decided to go along with her far-fetched plan to save the ranch by marrying a Remington.

Rome laughed. "Are you saying I've overstayed my welcome, Cloe?"

Before Cloe could reply, the humming grew louder. Mimi was coming into the barn. Cloe sent Rome a panicked look as she placed a finger against his lips. The only man's lips she had ever touched were Brandon's. They were thin and usually chapped. They weren't plump and soft and so warm that Cloe felt like she had just dipped her finger in perfectly heated bathwater. She jerked her hand away and stared at Rome as Mimi's humming grew louder.

The song was "Get Me to the Church On Time" from the musical *My Fair Lady*. Mimi loved musicals. Cloe had spent many a night as a kid cozied up in her grandmother's bed watching the fanciful shows.

The humming stopped right under the opening to the loft.

"Clover Fields! Are you up there? Your mama

has breakfast ready and you need to come get it before it gets cold."

Cloe pulled her gaze away from Rome and yelled down the opening. "I'm coming, Mimi. Don't come up. I don't want you to fall off the ladder."

As soon as the words were out of her mouth, she realized her mistake. Mimi loved to prove she was still spry. The creak of a foot stepping onto a ladder rung had Cloe glancing around frantically, looking for a place for Rome to hide. He took the decision from her by scooping up his hat and heading toward the open hatch doors.

She hurried after him. "You can't—" Before she could finish, he tugged on his hat, grabbed on to the lip of the hayloft hatch, and slipped over the edge. She leaned out and watched in horror as he dangled a good six feet off the ground. For a terrifying moment, he hung there before he dropped gracefully to his feet.

"Clover Fields Holiday, what are you doing hanging over that edge? Get back before you fall out!"

Cloe glanced over her shoulder to see her grandmother standing there with a concerned look on her face. Cloe looked back at Rome. The man had the audacity to blow her a kiss before he turned and jogged in the direction of the open field where all the townsfolk had parked for the wedding.

Once he was out of sight, Cloe turned to her grandmother and pinned on a smile. "Mornin', Mimi."

Mimi did not look happy. "What in the world are you doin' leaning out that hatch door? That was how your daddy broke his leg when he was eight."

"I wasn't leaning out that far. I was just looking for you. I heard you humming."

Mimi's eyes narrowed and Cloe was terrified she was going to be called out on the lie, but then, the mussed comforter and the champagne bucket caught her grandmother's attention. "What's all that?"

"I think Decker and Sweetie snuck up here during the reception for a little alone time."

Mimi chuckled. "That explains the hay in your sister's hair." Her gaze pinned Cloe. "But that doesn't explain why you slept up here?"

Cloe figured it was time to tell the truth. At least, about her engagement. "Brandon broke up with me and I needed some time alone."

"He broke your engagement?"

"There was no engagement. He never asked me to marry him. I guess that was just my wishful thinking."

Mimi sighed before she pulled Cloe into her arms and patted her back. "I'm sorry, Clover Fields. But things happen for a reason. I had a feeling Brandon wasn't a good match for you from the get-go."

Cloe drew back. "And how did you know that when you haven't even met him?"

"That right there was the first warning sign. If a man is interested in a woman, he's interested in her family. He didn't once come out to the ranch and meet your parents and me."

"Because my sisters put the fear of God in him about Daddy."

"Any man worth his salt wouldn't let a little fear stop him from doing what's right. Hallie said he was a wienie and I think she was onto something." Mimi gave her arms a squeeze. "But don't you fret, Clover Fields. You'll find the right man. God has a plan for you."

Cloe wished she could believe that. But at the moment, she felt like all her plans for the future had been erased in one fell swoop of Brandon's eraser and now she had nothing but a blank chalkboard . . . a blank life. She didn't have a boyfriend. Or a place to live. She still had her job, but she wasn't looking forward to returning to school after her leave of absence. She had already put in for a transfer, but that wouldn't happen until the following school year. Which meant she would have five weeks after she got back to College Station of trying to avoid Brandon in the teachers' lounge.

"Cloe! Mimi!" Liberty's voice carried up from the lower level of the barn and, a second later, her sister's head popped up through the opening in the floor. "Mimi, don't tell me you climbed this ladder. If Daddy finds out, he'll shit a brick."

"Watch your mouth, young lady. You'll never catch a man with a potty mouth. And I'm a grown woman who can climb a ladder if she wants to."

"And I'm a grown woman who has no desire to catch a man. Something I can't seem to get through my grandmother's thick skull." Liberty climbed the rest of the way up and rubbed her arms. "How did you spend the night up here, Clo? It's as cold as a well digger's as—butt."

An image of sleeping in the cocoon of Rome's hot body popped into her head and she felt her cheeks flame. Liberty squinted at her.

"Are you okay? You've been acting really weird lately. The entire thing with Rome on the side of the barn and then sleeping up here—"

Mimi cut her off. "What thing with Rome?"

"It was nothing," Cloe quickly said. "I was just feeling a little lightheaded and Rome helped me outside to get some fresh air."

"Belle said he helped her find you last night too," Liberty said.

Cloe was not a violent person, but she really wanted to sock her sister. Especially when Mimi was studying her with a gleam in her eyes. "Don't even think it, Mimi," she said. "Rome's just an honorable type of man. Now come on, y'all." She moved toward the ladder. "Mama won't be happy if breakfast gets cold." She and Mimi were almost to the ladder when Liberty's words stopped them.

"Whose tuxedo jacket is that?"

Cloe followed Liberty's gaze and saw a black tuxedo jacket draped over a bale of hay. Rome's tuxedo jacket. She hurried over and picked it up. "It must be Decker's. I'll make sure he gets it back. We wouldn't want him being charged extra by the tux rental for being late returning it." She didn't look at her sister or her grandmother as she quickly made her way down the ladder.

Once she got back to the house, she quickly headed upstairs to her room to hide the tuxedo jacket in her closet until she could get it back to Rome. But before she hung it on a hanger, she couldn't help holding it to her nose. It took numerous deep breaths before she could figure why Rome's scent was so familiar.

He smelled like hay, horses, saddle leather, and country air.

He smelled like home.

CHAPTER FIVE

"WHERE THE HELL have you been?"
Rome stopped on his way up the stairs and turned to see his father standing just outside his study. Sam Remington was an imposing man. It wasn't his size. At five foot ten inches and medium build, he was an average-sized man. His shoulders weren't broad or his belly big. But when he stepped into a room, people took notice.

It could have to do with his strong facial features: the prominent nose and high cheekbones he'd inherited from his great-great-grandmother who was full Sioux. The piercing gray eyes that missed nothing. The thick shock of black hair that had started turning gray when Rome was in high school and was now as silver as a shiny nickel.

Or maybe it was more the confident way he held himself. The aura of authority and arrogance that came with running one of the biggest ranches in Texas.

Swagger is what Casey called it.

Sam had swagger in spades.

And impatience.

"Well, answer the question, Roman."

"I just got home from Decker and Sweetie's wedding."

Sam glanced at his watch and then back at Rome. He didn't have to say a word to get his point across.

"I fell asleep in the hayloft," Rome explained.

Sam's eyes narrowed. "Alone."

"Actually, no." Rome had no intentions of elaborating. While his father hadn't said a word about him going to the Holidays' for the wedding, he would have more than a few choice words to say if he found out Rome had spent the night with a Holiday.

Not just any Holiday, but the wallflower of the Holiday sisters.

Except Cloe hadn't acted like a wallflower last night. Champagne had revealed a different woman beneath the reserved, and always controlled, façade. A woman who was more human and real . . . and sexy as hell.

It wasn't just the realization she'd been hiding some phenomenal breasts. Before he had even opened his eyes that morning, his body had reacted to the woman in his arms. The sweet scent of some kind of subtle perfume filled his lungs. Silky hair tickled his nose. Low rhythmic breathing soothed his ears. A soft, full bottom spooned in his lap.

When he'd opened his eyes, he'd glanced down to see Cloe sleeping contentedly with her auburn hair half covering her face. He'd smoothed it back and she'd wrinkled her cute little nose and grumbled in her sleep before grabbing his hand and cradling it to her chest like her favorite teddy bear.

Desire, hot and heavy, had settled inside him. He'd tried to will it down, but then she'd started wiggling that curvy butt against him. At that point, all he could think about was lifting her dress and sliding inside her warm heat from behind—of cradling her magnificent breasts as he pumped out the passion building inside him like an oil well ready to erupt.

Before he had done something stupid, he woke her.

"So you're telling me that you took a woman up to the Holidays' hayloft and had sex with her?" His father's annoyed voice cut into his thoughts. "During the reception?"

"Way to go, big bro!"

Rome glanced up. Casey stood at the top of the stairs looking like he'd just rolled out of bed. He wore nothing but his favorite Captain America boxers. His sandy hair stuck straight up and his light blue eyes were lit with a devilish light. He looked just like their mother. Glorieta'd had the same vibrancy and love of life . . . just not for her husband and sons.

"Good for you, Rome. It's about damn time you got back in the saddle."

Rome couldn't help the smile that spread over his face. His little brother had that ability. As soon as his mother and father brought Casey home, Rome had claimed him as his own. They were as close as two brothers could be.

That wasn't true about Sam and Casey's relationship. Sam loved Casey, but they had butted heads ever since Casey was old enough to state his mind. Annoying their father was something his brother lived for.

"And just what do you have to say about that, Sam? Now you have two sons who are—how did you put it? Oh, yeah. *Whoring around*."

Sam's face darkened. "And what exactly would you call your behavior with women?"

Casey grinned. "Enjoying what life has to offer." He looked at Rome and winked. "I'm glad my brother has joined me in that pursuit."

"It's one thing to enjoy what life has to offer," Sam said. "And it's another to ignore your responsibilities."

Casey's smile faded. "If I ignored my responsibilities, I wouldn't still be living here working my ass off every day."

"I'm not talking about the responsibilities to this ranch. I'm talking about your responsibilities to our family. It's time both of you settled down and had children who will carry on the Remington name. You won't find the kind of woman who will make a good wife and mother at the Hellhole." Sam looked at Rome. "Or in the Holidays' hayloft."

Like always, Casey stood up for him. "Well, you didn't find Mama in either place and look how that turned out."

Rome usually didn't step into his father and brother's verbal sparring unless blood was drawn. If the look on his father's face was any indication, it had been. One of Sam's strict rules was no discussing their mother. As a kid, Rome hadn't understood it. After Emily left him, now he did.

"Casey," Rome said. "That's enough."

Casey shrugged. "Just stating the truth. Glorieta came from a cream of the crop southern family. If she had come from lesser stock, she might have stayed." He looked at Sam. "Or did you lie about the reason she left and it had more to do with you than wanting to go back to her pampered life?"

"Don't push it, Casey," Sam said.

Casey knew when to call it quits. He looked back at Rome. "So who is the hayloft gal? Anyone I know?"

Rome shook his head. "Not going there."

Casey grinned. "I'll find out soon enough. There's no way to keep a secret in Wilder." He yawned widely and scratched his bare chest. "I'm going back to bed. That was one wild wedding."

Since Casey was the definition of wild, Rome wondered what had happened at the reception once he went into the hayloft. He started to follow his brother to ask when his father stopped him.

"Rome. I'd like to speak with you in my study."

Sam's study was a huge room off the main entrance, but with the dark décor and overly large furniture, it looked much smaller than it was. Wood was the main decorating element. The walls were paneled, the floors planked, and the furniture dark walnut. A stone fireplace occupied one wall; above its huge mantel hung a collection of longhorn bullhorns. The rest of the walls held original artwork from western artists—all of cowboys herding cattle on the Texas range. A bronze sculpture of a cowboy bronc-busting a wild mustang sat on the table between the two cowhide chairs that faced Sam's huge desk.

Rome took the chair he always took—the one closest to the door—and waited for his father to sit down behind the desk before he spoke.

"I hope you're not intending to give me a lecture, Daddy. I'm not sixteen anymore. You don't have to worry about me getting a girl pregnant."

"I'm not concerned about what happened in the hayloft—although there are still women out there who would love to trap a Remington into marriage."

"I thought that's what you wanted. Me to remarry and give you grandkids."

"With the right woman."

Rome sighed. "I told you I'm not getting married again. With the right or wrong woman."

"I know you were hurt badly when Emily left, but that doesn't mean you shouldn't try again."

Rome lifted his eyebrows. "You didn't."

"Because I already had you boys. There was no reason for me to remarry."

"What about companionship?"

Sam shrugged. "Like I said, I have you boys and the ranch." For Sam, that had always been enough. Over the years, he had dated different women in town, but he'd never brought those women home to meet his boys. Rome had learned about them through town gossip. There was a time when he had secretly wished for a mother. Not just for him, but for Casey. But as time went on, he'd grown up enough to realize his father was too hard a man to live with.

And maybe Rome was too. Maybe that's why Em had left.

Sam leaned back and rested his chin on his steepled fingers. "So how was the wedding?"

Since any show of weakness had never been tolerated, Rome figured his father wouldn't want to hear about his panic attack. "Good."

"I assume most of the town was there."

"Pretty much."

Sam snorted. "The Holidays can't afford to keep their ranch, and yet they can afford to throw the biggest wedding of the year."

"She's their daughter, Dad. You wanted me to have a big wedding."

"I have the money for it."

"According to Decker, it didn't cost them much. Bobby Jay donated the food. Sheryl Ann donated the cake. And Liberty and Belle are wedding planners so I'm sure they got everything else at cost."

"They shouldn't have spent any money when everyone knows they're two steps away from bankruptcy."

Rome mentally rolled his eyes. His father would never get over the feud he had going with Hank. Rome didn't know exactly what had started it. All he knew was that his father and Hank had a disagreement when they were young and never got over it. It colored his entire perspective of the

Holidays. If Rome was going to get the ranch, that needed to change.

"You're exaggerating," he said. "The Holidays aren't two steps away from bankruptcy. Just because they couldn't survive in the cattle business, they still have the ranch. They'll sell it and have plenty left over to live quite comfortably for the rest of their lives." Rome wasn't about to lowball them on his offer.

"They would be able to if Hank hadn't taken out so many loans."

Rome straightened. "How do you know he has loans?"

"It wasn't that hard to figure out. Every time a piece of land went up for sale, Hank was right there overbidding on it. I'm sure just to make sure I didn't get it. He took out one real estate contract after another with the surrounding ranchers. When he couldn't make the payments, he consolidated the loan. I'm sure at a high interest rate." Sam shook his head. "Hank never was a smart businessman. If he had been, he would have realized he was never cut out to be a cattleman. But his pride wouldn't let him. Now he'll be lucky to break even on the sale of the ranch."

So the Holidays' financial troubles were worse than he'd thought. Rome knew the Holiday Ranch had failed in the cattle business. It wasn't surprising given last year's drought and the price-gouging cattlemen had to deal with from the major packing companies. A lot of ranches had gone under. But he hadn't realized Hank was so in debt that the Holidays could lose everything.

"What will they do?" he asked. "How will Hank, Darla, and Ms. Mimi live?"

Sam shrugged. "I'm sure their daughters will take them in. I've heard that a couple of them are doing quite well for themselves. No doubt they got their mother's brains. But where the Holidays live is not our problem. Our problem is who they plan on selling the land to. I might not like Hank"—that was an understatement—"but I could count on him not to lease it to the government so they can put up a bunch of wind turbines. Or an oil company so they could drain it dry. Or even worse, sell it to some California idiot who has watched too many episodes of *Yellowstone* and wants to start his own dude ranch so he and his friends can play at being cowboys."

Rome tipped his head. "So, John Dutton, when do you want me to start killing people off?"

Sam didn't find his humor funny. "I hope it doesn't come to that," he said dryly.

Rome figured it was time to tell his father his plan. He would find out soon enough. "I want to buy the Holiday Ranch."

His father snorted. "Don't you think I've thought of that?"

Rome was surprised. "I thought you didn't want anything that belonged to Hank."

A sad look entered his father's eyes, but it was gone so quickly Rome figured he was mistaken. "I don't. But if I thought Hank would accept, I'd buy the ranch—if only to keep from having idiot neighbors. But he will never sell to a Remington."

"He won't sell to you. But it's possible he might sell to me. That's if I can convince him I want to run the ranch on my own." He thought his father would throw a fit, but Sam seemed to think his desire to run the ranch alone was all a ruse to get the Holiday Ranch.

"You think Hank will fall for it?"

Rome started to tell the truth and then decided to wait. Sam didn't share all his plans with Rome. Rome figured he didn't need to share all his plans with his father. "All I can do is try. Maybe I'll even tell him I'll keep the name Holiday Ranch."

"Like hell you will!"

"If a Remington owns it, what difference does a name make?"

"A lot of difference. I'd just as soon the Holiday name disappeared from this county."

Rome asked the question he'd asked at least a hundred times. "What happened between you and Hank?" He got the same answer.

"None of your damn business. So when are you making Hank an offer?"

"I don't think there's any hurry. It's not even on the market yet." He got to his feet. "Now I'm going to take a shower."

Before he got to the door, Sam stopped him. "So who was the girl in the hayloft?"

An image popped into Rome's mind. An image of curls the color of deep burgundy apples and eyes the color of late summer grass . . . and breasts so full and soft they'd tempt a saint.

"Just a girl."

CHAPTER SIX

"I DON'T KNOW WHY we were stuck wash-ing all the reception dishes?"

Cloe stopped drying the plate and glanced at Noelle who was washing dishes at the sink. Noelle was the baby of the family. And there had never been a more adorable baby. Noelle had always been chubby and full cheeked with the Holiday green eyes and Mimi's bowed lips and button nose. She had long eyelashes that any woman would kill for and dimples that creased both cheeks whenever she smiled.

She was like a perfect little doll.

Which probably explained why everyone in the family had spoiled her rotten. Everyone but Daddy. He didn't believe in spoiling any of his girls. Although recently, he had become more approachable. Cloe wasn't sure if it had to do with him getting into so much debt he was going to lose his ranch or his heart attack.

Her father had almost died two months earlier when he'd suffered a heart attack while fixing a broken fence. Luckily, Rome had discovered him and called 911. Otherwise, her daddy might not be there.

Just the thought of Rome had her body flushing with heat as a flood of memories filled her brain. Memories of ruffled dark hair and sleepy gray eyes. Memories of a strip of naked, well-defined chest dusted with hair . . . and an extremely hard erection. She didn't understand her body's reactions. She had never had these kind of heated thoughts about Brandon. Not even after their scheduled Saturday night lovemaking.

And yet, just the thought of Rome's hard body pressing against her made her feel like a boiling pan of hot caramel.

"Did I miss some barbecue sauce on that plate?"

Noelle's question pulled her from her wayward thoughts and she realized she had stopped drying the plate and was just standing there staring at it. She shook her head and continued drying. "I was just woolgathering."

Noelle sent her a compassionate look. "I'm sorry about Brandon breaking up with you, Clo." Cloe had told her entire family, besides Sweetie and Decker who were enjoying their honeymoon, about the breakup over breakfast. They'd all had different reactions. Mama and Belle had hugged her close while Daddy, Liberty, and Hallie had wanted to hunt him down and make him pay. Noelle hadn't said much until now. "I guess you can't help thinking about him."

That should be the case. After all, Brandon was her one and only boyfriend. But since waking up with Rome, Brandon hadn't entered Cloe's mind once. While it was a relief, it was also disconcerting. What was wrong with her? She should be thinking about a man she'd been with for six long years. She certainly shouldn't be thinking about a man she barely knew.

"I'm fine, Elle," she said as she stacked the plate in the box with the rest of the clean plates. "Now tell me about your latest TikTok recipe."

Noelle attended a pastry school in Dallas and spent all her free time posting her recipes on Tik-Tok hoping to become a social media sensation. And she *had* built quite a following.

"You really need to get on TikTok, Clo, and then I wouldn't have to tell you about my posts."

"You know I'm not much of a social media person." She didn't even have a Facebook account.

"I know." Noelle shook her head. "And it's pure craziness. There's an entire world out there that you're missing out on. Take online dating, for example. Nowadays, you can find a new boyfriend with just a swipe of your phone." She quickly grabbed a dish towel and dried her hands. "In fact, let's get you signed up on a dating app right now."

Cloe held up her hand. "No, thank you, Elle. I might be fine, but I'm not ready to get back into the dating scene just yet."

"Why not? Daddy always taught us that when you fall off a horse you need to get right back in the saddle."

Once again, Cloe couldn't help thinking about the way her bottom had fit so perfectly in Rome's lap. It had felt like sitting in her favorite well-worn saddle.

"What's the holdup, ladies?" Liberty barreled into the room. "The rest of us have cleaned the entire barn while it looks like you two have been dawdling."

"Dawdling?" Noelle glared at her. "You try washing a thousand plates, glasses, and eating utensils. My hands are so water wrinkled they look like Mimi's and my polish is chipping like the old paint on the chicken coop." She held up her hands. "How am I supposed to do cooking videos with hands that look like these?"

"Oh, no!" Liberty dramatically held a hand to her chest. "Chipped polish? What a TikTok disaster." She lowered her hand and shook her head. "I swear you are so egotistical, Elle, it's not even funny."

"I am not egotistical. I just like my hands to look their best when I do my posts. And don't act like you don't primp, Libby. I've seen your closet of designer clothes and shoes."

"As a successful businesswoman, I need to wear stylish clothes. It's all about the first impression, kid." Liberty waved a hand at the old T-shirt and faded jeans she wore. "But if you'll note, when I'm doing messy jobs, I dress appropriately and don't worry about my nails."

Noelle glanced down at her pink sweater and tight blue jeans. "I'm dressed appropri—oh, no, I got some of Bobby Jay's barbecue sauce on my sweater and I just bought it. I need to get some prewash on it before it stains." She hurried out of the kitchen.

When she was gone, Liberty took over at the sink and wasted no time rinsing the pile of forks, spoons, and knives. "That girl needs to do some major growing up."

"We all did when we were her age." Cloe finished boxing the plates and reached for the packing tape to seal up the box.

"Not you, Clo. You've always been responsible. Something I've always admired."

Cloe hadn't been very responsible last night. What had she been thinking getting drunk and letting some man spoon her? Of course, she was lucky it had been Rome who found her and not some other man. Rome had always been trust-worthy and honorable. It didn't hurt that he had never found her attractive.

The memory of his hard length pressing against her popped into her head again, but she pushed it away. His erection had just been a morning hard-on. Brandon had gotten those . . . just not quite as big.

"I'm sorry about Brandon, Clo."

Liberty's words pulled her from her thoughts and she glanced at her sister to find Liberty had turned away from the sink and was watching Cloe with concerned eyes.

"I guess that explains why you were so upset at the wedding." Liberty's eyes darkened. "Are you sure you don't want to go to College Station and key his car? Or maybe set it on fire? The asshole more than deserves it for stringing you along for six years."

Liberty's blunt honesty could really hurt at times. "I don't think he meant to. I think it just took him that long to figure out I wasn't the right woman for him."

Liberty's temper flared. "Not the right woman for him? That asshole wasn't good enough for you. He was lucky you even gave him the time of day. And I hope you told him that. I hope you lit into him and told him that you were the best thing to ever happen to him and it will be a cold day in hell before he finds someone as dependable, hardworking, and organized as you."

"Thank you, but I don't think dependable, hardworking, and organized are top of any man's list when looking for a wife."

"Well, they should be. And I don't want you thinking any less of yourself because Brandon couldn't see your worth. I didn't want to say this when you had your heart set on marrying him, but I never did think he was worthy of you. As far as I'm concerned, you're better off without him."

That was easy for Liberty to say. Liberty had always been the most popular Holiday sister. She was beautiful and outgoing and commanding. When she walked into a room, men and women alike sat up and took notice. Women wanted to be her best friend and men fell at her feet and groveled for just a simple smile.

Cloe, on the other hand, could walk into a room and no one would notice. She had always been fine with that. She had never liked a lot of attention. But a lot and none were two different things.

That was why Brandon had been her first real boyfriend. Conversing with men was just another thing she didn't excel at. But with Brandon, they had so much in common, conversation had come easily. He had made her feel comfortable and their life together had taken on a nice routine. There was nothing Cloe loved better than routine. They drove to work together. They drove back to their apartment together. He rode his Peloton while she cooked dinner. Then they ate, graded papers or worked on lesson plans, and then went to bed. Every Saturday night they had sex.

Occasionally, it had felt like something was missing. But only occasionally. Now she realized that something had been missing. She just had been too stupid to realize it.

"I got the stain out." Noelle walked back into the kitchen.

Liberty stared at the sweater Noelle had changed into. "White, Elle?" She shook her head and snorted. "And you were a straight-A student."

Once everything was washed and boxed up, Cloe helped Liberty and Noelle carry the boxes out to Liberty's SUV. They were loading them into the back when Cloe heard the sound of a car coming up the road. She figured it was either Daddy's or Hallie's truck. Mama, Daddy, Hallie, and Belle had gone into town to return the chairs and tables they'd borrowed from the First Baptist Church for the wedding.

The car that pulled up in behind Liberty's SUV *was* a truck.

It just wasn't Daddy's or Hallie's.

This truck was big and black with huge tires and plenty of shiny chrome . . . and a front license plate that had the Remington Ranch's double R brand on it.

There was only one reason Cloe could think of for Rome being there.

He had come for his tuxedo jacket.

Not only did she not want Mimi to know she and Rome spent the night together in the hayloft, she also didn't want her sisters knowing. She didn't worry about them telling Mimi. They had all taken an oath long ago to keep each other's secrets. What she worried about was setting a bad example for her sisters. And spending the night in the hayloft with a man you barely knew was setting a bad example.

So before Rome even got both brown cowboy boots on the ground, Cloe was there to greet him.

"Rome! What a surprise."

He looked a little startled by her exuberant greeting. Probably because Cloe had never been exuberant in her life.

"Uhh . . . hey." He swept off his hat. "I just stopped by to—"

Once again, Cloe pressed a finger to his lips. Once again, the mere touch heated her body like a gust of late August wind. She jerked her hand back.

"No need to explain. A man who saved my

daddy's life doesn't need a reason to stop by."
She grabbed his arm—maybe a little too tightly
because he flinched—and pulled him toward
the porch steps. "Come on into the house and
I'll get you something to drink and a piece of
leftover wedding cake while you wait for Mama
and Daddy to get back from town. I'm sure they
won't be long."

As she tugged him past Liberty and Noelle, she
prayed her sisters wouldn't say anything. They
didn't. They both seemed to be as stunned by her
uncharacteristic behavior as Rome was. Once
inside, she dropped his arm and tried to explain.

"I'm sorry, but it would be better if my sisters didn't know we spent the night together. Or
about me getting drunk and acting foolish." Cloe
glanced out the window. Liberty and Noelle
were in deep discussion—no doubt about Cloe's
uncharacteristic behavior. They both probably
thought she had lost her mind over the breakup.

Maybe she had.

She certainly felt off kilter when she looked
back at Rome and found him studying her with
his soft gray eyes.

"You didn't do anything to be ashamed of,
Cloe. It's okay to blow off a little steam every
now and then. Especially after what you've been
through."

She had thought Rome being so nice to her
last night had to do with him wanting a distrac-
tion from his wedding memories. But here he
was today being just as nice. She didn't know
what to make of it.

She self-consciously tucked a strand of loose hair behind her ear and cleared her throat. "Still, I'd appreciate it if you didn't tell anyone. I'll drop your tuxedo jacket by later today."

"Actually, I'm not worried about the jacket. I just stopped by to see how you were feeling this morning."

"Oh. Well, I'm feeling fine, thank you."

He squinted at her. "You sure? Or is that just the standard reply you give everyone? Because I wouldn't be fine if I'd just broken up with a girl I'd dated since college, my family was losing their ranch, and I was hungover as hell. I don't think anyone would be."

She started to argue the point and then realized there was no argument. He was right. She wasn't okay. "I guess I've had better days."

"You want to talk about it?"

"There's nothing to talk about. Brandon broke up with me. The ranch has to be sold. I drank too much champagne and my body is paying for it today. End of story."

He studied her for a moment. "I wish it was that easy to compartmentalize problems and push our feelings aside, but I think we both know that's not how it works. Sometimes, you just need to get those feelings out. And I get that you can't talk to your family because you don't want to worry them." He shrugged. "But you can talk to me."

She didn't get what was happening here and she couldn't pretend any longer that she did. "I'm sorry, but I don't understand. We've never been friends, Rome, and now suddenly you're acting like we are."

He looked taken back. "Not friends? I disagree with you. We've known each other all our lives. You shared pencils and your lunch with me in grade school. Tutored me in geometry and helped me ace that final in high school. And came to my rescue when I was having a panic attack. Now if that's not a good friend, I don't know what is."

"That's just what people do. We don't really know each other."

"Of course we do. I bet you know more about me than you think. What kind of trucks do I like?"

Once again, she didn't understand where he was going with all this. "This is silly."

"So you don't know."

"Of course I know. One's parked out front. Dodge Rams."

"And what color was my first truck?"

"Again easy because you've only ever driven one color truck. Black." She hesitated. "No—I take that back. When Casey stole your truck his freshman year and ran it into Mr. Fletcher's mailbox, you had to drive that white rental truck. But everyone knew you hated every second of it."

"I'm not a white truck kind of guy. And that right there proves you know me."

"Just because I know what color trucks you drive doesn't mean anything. You were one of the most popular boys in town when we were growing up. Everyone knew what you drove and that you like Tony Lama boots and JW Brooks Custom Hats and Hanes underwear." She cringed when she realized what had slipped out.

He stared at her. "You know what kind of underwear I wear?"

Her cheeks flamed as she looked away. "I . . . umm . . . it was just girls' locker-room gossip. I don't know for sure."

A big smile split his face. "Like I said. You know me. And I know you."

"Really? What car did I drive?"

"You didn't have a car until you left for college and if I remember correctly it was a used Chevy Cavalier. In high school, you drove to school with your sister Sweetie in Mustang Sally that she got for her sixteenth birthday. Our senior year you drove to school with Liberty and Belle in the car they got for their sixteenth birthdays." He cocked his head. "I often wondered why you didn't get a car for your sixteenth."

"I didn't want one. I thought it was silly for Daddy and Mama to spend the money on a car when I never went anywhere and I was fine driving to school with my sisters."

He studied her. "You've always been practical. Which probably explains why you were the one who started the campaign to get Wilder High students to start recycling their cans and water bottles. The one who organized the prom dress swap every year . . . even though you never went. Why was that? Your sisters went."

"I don't dance."

His eyes twinkled. "You wanted to last night."

She covered her face with her hands. "Please don't remind me of what I did last night."

"Why? I thought you were cute."

She lowered her hands and looked at him. "Proof you don't know me. I've never been cute in my life."

"Now there you're wrong. You're cute every time you wrinkle your nose to get your glasses to slip back up." To her total embarrassment, her nose did exactly what he'd just said. He laughed and reached out to tap it. "Cute. And you were cute when you dressed up like the Cat in the Hat in fourth grade."

"That was all Liberty's idea. She wanted her and Belle to go as Thing One and Thing Two and she begged me to go as the Cat. And I wasn't cute. I looked like a skinny drowned alley cat."

"You *were* pretty skinny back then. You still are." His gaze lowered to her breasts. "In some places." Before she could get over the fact that Rome was checking her out, his gaze lifted and he continued with the crazy questioning. "What's my favorite muffin at Nothin' But Muffins? You always order Wild Blueberry Hill."

She was shocked he knew what muffin she ordered. She wanted to pretend like she didn't know his, but she knew. Wascally Wabbit Carrot with cream cheese glaze. He licked the glaze off first before he carefully peeled off the wrapper and ate the muffin in four neat bites. In high school, he always ordered two muffins with three bottles of 2 percent milk.

"Okay." She held up her hands in defeat. "We

know each other, but that doesn't explain why you're here."

He paused before he spoke. "Maybe it's nice to hang out with someone who understands what I've been through."

She couldn't argue with that. He was right. It would be nice to hang out with someone who understood what she was going through. Someone who knew what it felt like to have your heart broken in two and not know how to put it back together. But Rome Remington? He was the last person in the world she would have thought would want to be her friend.

"It's supposed to be a clear night tomorrow," he said. "I thought I'd do a little stargazing. You want to join me? Noelle told me last night that all your sisters are heading home tomorrow. I figure you might be a little lonely."

It was true. Noelle was heading back to Dallas this afternoon. Hallie planned to leave for Austin in the morning . And Liberty and Belle would leave for Houston soon after. Sweetie was living in Wilder now, but she and Decker were in Nashville honeymooning and packing up Sweetie's apartment. Still, Cloe wouldn't be lonely. She'd have Mama, Daddy, and Mimi to keep her company. Although they usually were in bed by eight.

"Where are you planning on stargazing?" she asked.

"I'm thinking Cooper Springs?" A smile split Rome's face. "But we'll need to get permission from the landowner first."

Cooper Springs? The last time she'd been

at Cooper Springs was when she'd gone skinny-dipping with her sisters as part of the Holiday Secret Sisterhood's full-moon ritual that had been started when they were just kids. Rome and Decker had shown up. Thankfully, it had been night and Rome had been a gentleman and swam off as soon as he realized the sisters were naked.

Which proved he could be trusted.

"What time do you want to meet?" she asked.

"How about around ten?"

She nodded. "I'll bring your tuxedo jacket."

"No hurry. It's not rented." He tugged on his hat. "I guess I'll see you tomorrow night."

Once he was gone, Cloe stood there for a moment trying to figure out what had just happened. Had she just agreed to become Rome's friend?

It looked like she had.

She shook her head as she turned to the kitchen to see if they had left any boxes of dishes. She startled when she saw Mimi standing on the stairs. She looked like she had just woken up from a nap. Her puff of white hair was smashed on one side and deep pillow creases marred one cheek. But her eyes were alert and twinkling.

"So I guess that wasn't Decker's tuxedo jacket after all."

CHAPTER SEVEN

"LET ME GET this straight." Casey turned in his saddle to look at Rome. "You're befriending Cloe Holiday so you can get information that will give you an edge on buying the Holiday Ranch."

Rome cringed. Put that way, it made him sound like their father. "I'm not befriending Cloe Holiday just because I want information on the ranch. I like Cloe. I've always liked her."

"If that's true, then why haven't you made any attempt to be her friend before this?" When Rome struggled to find an answer, Casey snorted. "I thought so."

Rome adjusted the reins in his hand and rode around a pothole. "Okay, so maybe I didn't make an attempt to be friends with her in high school. But now that I've gotten to know her a little, I'd like to be her friend. We have a lot in common. We both grew up on ranches with stubborn Texas daddies. We attended the same schools. Know the same people."

"Both got dumped by your significant others."

Rome shot him an annoyed look. "Thanks for the reminder."

Casey grinned. "That's what brothers are for. So what you're trying to tell me is it's okay that you're using Cloe because you're going to grace her with your friendship." Shit. Why did Casey always have to put things in perspective? "I get it," he continued. "You want to get out from under Daddy's thumb and buying the Holiday Ranch is the perfect solution. You can still help run this ranch, but from a distance." He shot him a look. "I hope there will be room in that big ol' farmhouse for your little brother because I'm not living with Daddy without our mediator. We'd kill each other."

Rome nodded. "There will always be room in my house for you, little brother."

"Then why don't you just tell Cloe about your interest in buying her family's ranch. She seems like a logical, practical girl. From what I hear, they need to sell quickly and for as much as they can get for it."

"Where did you hear that?"

Casey grinned. "I never divulge my sources. So I'm assuming Cloe was the woman you seduced in the hayloft."

"I didn't seduce her. We just fell asleep. There was no touching. Just talking."

But even as he said the words, an image popped into his head of his hand pressed to soft, abun-dant breasts . . . followed by the moment when he'd actually been about to kiss her. Thankfully, Mimi's humming had interrupted them. If he had kissed her, he would be struggling even more to justify his plan of becoming friends with Cloe.

"Wanting to be her friend is not all about getting information from her," he said. "She's been through a lot and doesn't seem to have anyone to talk to. Her sisters are all busy with their own lives and I happen to understand how devastating getting . . . dumped can be."

They rode for a few minutes before Casey spoke. "Maybe it would be good for you and Cloe to become friends. I think you still have a lot of pent-up anger over Emily that you need to get out."

"I don't have pent-up anger over Emily."

Casey shook his head. "Sure you don't. That's why you haven't dated since she left."

"I've dated."

"You've had a few one-night stands right after Emily left. That's not dating. That's sex. And you haven't even been with a woman for three years." Casey looked completely bewildered. "Three. Years."

"I've been busy."

"If you're too busy for sex, you're too busy. I love this ranch too, Romy, but that doesn't mean I'm going to let it keep me from enjoying life."

"Nothing keeps you from enjoying life."

Casey grinned. "True. Maybe you need to take a page out of your little brother's book." His smile faded. "I get it, Rome. You loved her and she broke your heart, but that doesn't mean you should give up on women. There's someone else out there for you. I know it."

Positivity was just something else he loved about his little brother. Casey never let anything bring him down. He also wasn't realistic. If he wanted something, he never thought things through. He just went for it full steam ahead. To hell with the consequences. Rome, on the other hand, thought everything through. He listed pros and cons and took plenty of time before he made his decision. The only time he hadn't done that was with love. When he fell for Emily, he hadn't thought, he'd just dove right in.

And look at how that turned out.

But never again.

"Like I told you before, Case," he said. "I'm not interested in getting married again. Carrying on the Remington name and making Daddy happy is all up to you, little bro."

Casey laughed. "Then I guess the Remington name will end with us. Because the last thing I enjoy doing is making Sam happy." He shot a challenging look over at Rome. "Race you home?" Before the words were even out of Casey's mouth, Rome was urging his horse into a gallop.

When Cloe didn't show up at Cooper Springs by ten thirty that night, Rome should have headed home and left well enough alone. Casey was right. Rome shouldn't be using Cloe to get information about the ranch. But on the way back to his truck, he started to get worried.

The springs were walking distance from the

Holidays' house. What if Cloe had decided to walk? There were plenty of dangers on a ranch. During the day, you could watch out for snakes or potholes. At night, it wasn't as easy. Figuring he'd just check to make sure she wasn't lying hurt somewhere, he got a flashlight from his truck and scanned the area between the springs and the house.

Thankfully, he didn't find Cloe. But that didn't appease his concern. Especially when he noticed the light on in the upstairs window. It had to be Cloe's. Her other sisters had left and he'd learned while getting ready for Sweetie and Decker's wedding that her parents' bedroom was on the main floor. He couldn't see her grandmother staying up this late.

So if Cloe was up, why hadn't she met him? Was she hiding in her room with a broken heart?

A trellis stood next to the window, covered in some kind of thick vines. Rome set down his flashlight and starting climbing. Halfway up, his brain kicked in and questioned his stupidity. The trellis was more than a little wobbly. Still, his curiosity got the best of him and he kept going. When he reached the window, he leaned over and peeked in. He barely registered the gardening hats hanging on hooks by the door when the window was thrown open and he was whacked on the head with something that hurt like hell.

"Pervert!"

Rome lost his footing, but still had a tight hold on the trellis. Unfortunately, his dangling weight proved too much for the fragile structure. With the sound of snapping vines, the trellis slowly started falling away from the house, Rome clinging to it like a scared squirrel to a broken limb. He hit the ground on his back, thankful for the thick lining of his sheepskin jacket. But it still knocked the air out of him. While he lay there with the trellis on him struggling to breathe, a beam of light came toward him, causing him to squint when it hit his eyes.

"Rome Remington?" Mimi said. "What in the world are you doing?" While Rome struggled to catch his breath, she figured it out on her own. "You thought it was Cloe's room, didn't you?" She didn't sound at all angry. In fact, she chuckled with delight before she removed the light from his eyes and leaned closer. "You okay?"

"Y-Y-Yes, m-m-ma'am." The words squeaked out of his mouth like slowly released air from a balloon.

"Knocked the wind out of ya, did it? I've had that happen a time or two. Give it a second and you should be fine. Although we should probably get that trellis off you." Even though he was struggling to breathe, he didn't want her trying to lift the heavy trellis by herself so he summoned enough strength to shove it off. She kept the light in his eyes the entire time. "You want to tell me what went on in that hayloft with my granddaughter? Cloe claimed it was nothing. But if that's so, then why are you trying to sneak into her room?"

"I-I-I w-w-wasn't sneaking." He sat up and

took a deep breath before he continued. "We were supposed to meet at Cooper Springs to stargaze, but she didn't show up. I wanted to make sure she was okay."

"So that's why she isn't in her room."

She wasn't there? Damn. He must have missed her on the way over.

He squinted in the light. "Do you think you could not shine that in my eyes, Ms. Mimi?"

She turned off the flashlight. It took a second for his eyes to adjust. Mimi stood there looking down at him with her white hair glowing like a half moon around her head. She wore a coat that hung open to reveal a WWE T-shirt with some screaming male wrestler on the front and a pair of flannel pajama bottoms that were tucked into rubber gardening boots with handles on the sides.

"Looks like you're going to be fine," she said.

He didn't know about fine. The aches in his body said he'd have more than a few bruises in the morning. He slowly got to his feet and picked up his hat. "I'm sorry to have bothered you, Ms. Mimi. I better go see where Cloe is. I'm sure she's waiting for me at Cooper Springs." He started to leave, but Mimi stopped him.

"She can wait. I'd like to know your intentions with my granddaughter."

Rome held up his hand. "My intentions are honorable. Cloe and I are just friends."

"Are you telling me there's no hanky-panky going on?"

"None." Besides the accidental spooning and almost kiss. But he figured she didn't need to know about those. "Cloe and I just struck up a friendship at the wedding."

"So what did you do all night in the hayloft?"

"Slept."

Mimi snorted. "That's the same story I got from Cloe."

"Because it's true."

Mimi sighed. "Well, that's not what I was hoping to hear, but I guess being comfortable enough to sleep together is better than nothing. Of course, if you had had sex, we could have used the pregnant card so her daddy wouldn't put up such a fuss when we tell him about you two getting married. After you saved his life, he doesn't hate you anymore. But he sure doesn't like you either."

Rome blinked, thinking that maybe he'd suffered a concussion in the fall. "Excuse me? What did you just say?"

"You didn't know that Hank doesn't like you?"

Rome shook his head. "No, the other part. You think Cloe and I are getting married?"

"Is there another reason you've been following her around like a little lost puppy? You haven't exactly shown interest in her over the years. Don't get me wrong. I'm not mad at you for it—I know what a treasure Cloe is. But most folks don't. Mostly, because she hasn't discovered her worth yet. But mark my words, she will. When she does, she will shine brighter than those stars hanging over your head. But I figure, right now, your only interest in her is to get your hands on this ranch."

Damn. The woman was much more perceptive than he'd thought.

"Don't look so surprised that I figured it out," she said. "After all, I'm the one who made you the offer."

Until now, Rome hadn't given much thought to the text he'd received from Mimi over a month ago. At first, he'd thought it was a prank. But then, Decker had told him Mimi really had sent the text. She'd sent one to Casey too. They'd both had a good laugh over Mimi's audacity, but Rome had also thought it was sweet. She loved her granddaughters and wanted them to move closer to her. You didn't get any closer than the Remington Ranch. Rome hated to be the one to crush her dream. But there was no way around it.

"I'm sorry, Ms. Mimi. But I'm not going to marry Cloe. I'm never getting married again."

"Not even for this ranch?"

He cleared his throat. "I don't think this is your ranch to give."

"Like hell it's not. My name is on the deed."

Talk about feeling like he'd just had the wind knocked out of him. All he could do was stare at the little woman and try to speak. "W-W-What?"

"While my son runs this ranch, I'm the one who owns it. Every last acre."

"So you're the one selling this ranch?"

"Hell, no, I'm not selling it!"

He was struggling to understand. "But I thought the ranch was in debt."

"According to what Cloe tells me, up to the

barn's rooftop. But I don't care. Let the loan shark my son tricked me into signing a loan with try to repossess this ranch and he'll find himself staring down the end of my husband's shotgun. This is Holiday land and it will remain Holiday land. If not in my name, then in the name of my great-grandchildren's daddy—once he pays off the debt and we get the title back. If that daddy isn't going to be you, I figure your brother will be smart enough to take me up on my offer."

Rome was too stunned to do more than stare at her in disbelief.

"Rome? Mimi? What's going on?"

Rome turned to see Cloe walking toward them. She was bundled up in a knee-length puffy coat and a knit beanie that covered most of her hair. Those green eyes zeroed in on him. "I went to Cooper Springs, but you weren't there. Did I misunderstand where we were meeting?"

"I was there. We must have missed each other. I came here to see if you were okay."

"And ended up climbing our trellis and breaking it," Mimi said.

Cloe glanced at the trellis lying on the ground. "You climbed my grandmother's honeysuckle trellis?"

"I thought it was your window. Your grandmother made me realize my mistake."

Mimi sniffed. "I thought it was some pervert trying to get a peek so I whacked him over the head with my Bible."

A smile broke over Cloe's face and her dimples popped for a brief second before she bit her plump bottom lip and tried not to laugh. "Are you okay?"

Mimi answered for him. "He's fine, but he probably should get on home and take a couple aspirins."

He knew when he was being dismissed and Mimi was right. He did need some aspirins. Not to mention, time to absorb what he'd just learned. Mimi owned the ranch?

"It is late," Cloe said. "I guess we'll have to star-gaze another night."

Mimi shook her head. "Absolutely not. Not when Rome has just informed me he's not inter-ested in marriage. Therefore, he's not welcome to stargaze with my granddaughter."

Cloe eyes widened. "Mimi!"

"Don't you *Mimi* me, Clover Fields Holiday. Rome is after something with all his trellis-climb-ing and wedding-flirting, but it's not anything decent. I won't have you giving away the apple-cart without it being paid for."

Cloe closed her eyes and groaned. Rome fig-ured it was time to make his exit. He tugged on his hat. "I best be going. Good night, ladies."

He headed back the way he'd come, his mind a swirl of thoughts. Mimi owned the ranch and had no intentions of selling it. But it sounded like she didn't have a choice if foreclosure was an option. No wonder she had come up with the crazy plan to marry off one of her grand-daughters. She was desperate to keep a ranch that had been in her family for over a century. Rome knew he would do whatever was necessary to save his family's ranch. But he couldn't see any of the sisters being willing to go along with their grandmother's ridiculous plan.

Suddenly, he pictured Cloe dressed in a cat suit with a tie and a top hat, miserably trailing behind Thing One and Thing Two. Cloe standing at the Hellhole bar sipping a Dr Pepper and looking like she'd rather be anywhere else while Hallie and Sweetie drank, danced, and flirted. Cloe with a bright smile pinned on her face as she fixed Sweetie's veil and fluffed the trail of her wedding dress—all while Cloe's own heart was broken.

He realized he was wrong.

There was one sister who would go along with any plan that benefited her family.

Now the only question was, would he?

CHAPTER EIGHT

CLOE HAD NEVER been to the Remington Ranch, but that hadn't stopped her from imagining what a wealthy rancher's house would look like. As she parked her car in front, she realized her imagination had been way off.

She had envisioned a grand ranch-style home fitting one of the biggest ranchers in the county. But the two-story brick house was smaller than her family's farmhouse ... and not nearly as homey. There were no bright flower gardens bordering the front. No cozy swing and patio furniture on the porch. No pretty shutters and window boxes to add color to the bland off-white Austin stone. Probably because the Remingtons had no women to add all those cozy touches.

Which meant they didn't know the joy of seeing flowers bloom in a profusion of colors, or the calming peace of sitting on a porch swing and watching the brilliant sunset fade into twilight.

They didn't know what a home could be.

The thought made her sad. She was still standing there looking at the house when the front door opened and Sam Remington stepped out onto the porch. He looked like Rome. Or Rome looked like him. He wasn't as tall or broad shouldered as his son, but the facial features were the same. With his silver hair, he looked like the actor James Brolin. Like Rome, his eyes pinned her with their smoky intensity.

"Can I help you?"

She moved up the porch steps with an outstretched hand. "Hello, Mr. Remington. I'm Cloe Holiday."

He shook her hand. "I knew you were a Holiday. Your eyes are a dead giveaway."

She smiled. "It's a family trait. Eyes from my mama and our stubbornness from our daddy."

Sam snorted, but didn't comment. "So what brings you here, Miss Holiday?"

"I was wondering if Rome was home. And please call me Cloe."

"He's out on the range at the moment. Is there something I can help you with?"

She held out the tuxedo jacket she'd forgotten to take with her to Cooper Springs. "I wanted to return his jacket. He left it at the wedding." Although that wasn't the only reason she'd come.

Sam's eyes registered surprise and she didn't know if it was over his son forgetting his jacket or a Holiday returning it. He took it with a nod. "Thank you. I'll make sure he gets it." He studied her. "You have your mother's cheekbones and chin too." It was true, but she was surprised he was so familiar with her mother's features that he could make the comparison. Of course, they had attended high school together. "I hear your father is selling the ranch," he continued, pulling her away from her thoughts.

She wasn't sure how to answer. She had thought her grandmother had finally realized they had to sell the ranch. Last night had proven her wrong. Mimi was more adamant than ever about keeping the ranch. Rome showing up and climbing the trellis had given her hope that her plan to marry one of her granddaughters off to a Remington was going to work . . . even if Rome had made it clear he didn't want to get married. Which was why Cloe was there. She wanted to apologize and make sure Rome knew she had no part in her grandmother's scheme.

"Hey, Cloe!"

She turned to find Casey walking from the stables with a big, welcoming smile. She had always liked Casey. Although most women did. He was a rascally charmer who had a way of making every woman feel like they had his full attention.

"So what brings you to Casa Remington?" He pulled off his cowboy hat as he climbed the steps of the porch, revealing his mussed golden locks. "Please tell me you're here to see me and not my boring brother. Rome never has known what to do with a beautiful woman."

She couldn't help laughing. "Sorry, but I'm here to see Rome. And since I've never been beautiful that works out just fine."

"Not beautiful? You must not own a mirror."

His father interrupted his son's outrageous flirting. "Did you get that new mare taken care of, Casey?"

Casey didn't even glance at his father. "Of course, Sam. Your wish is always my command." He held out his arm. "Come on, Cloe. I'll take you to Rome."

She glanced at Sam as they headed down the porch steps. "It was nice meeting you, Mr. Remington."

He merely nodded.

Once they were away from the house, Casey apologized. "You'll have to pardon my daddy. We don't get much company. So what brings you to the devil's lair?"

"I need to talk to your brother and I should probably talk to you too. I don't doubt for a second you'll be getting another text or phone call from my grandmother about marrying one of her granddaughters in exchange for the ranch."

Casey grinned. "She's still matchmaking, huh? Well, you have to give it to her. She's not a quitter."

"No. She's as stubborn as my daddy. Although her renewed interest in marrying us off is all my fault."

Casey quirked an eyebrow. "Does this have anything to do with you spending the night with my brother in the hayloft?"

She blinked at him, surprised Rome had told him. "I hope he told you nothing happened."

"He did. But even if he hadn't, I would have figured it out." He hesitated. "Rome's had a hard time of it after Emily left him. He's not quite ready to get back in the saddle." He winked at her. "But he might be getting there."

She knew what he was implying and she shook her head. "Oh, no. It's not like that between us. We're just . . ." Not sure exactly what they were, she left the sentence hanging.

Casey grinned. "Well, I hope you stay around long enough to fill in that blank."

He led her to the Remingtons' large stables where she expected to find Rome. Instead, the only ones to greet her were a friendly dog, a not-so-friendly goat, and some lazy barn cats that refused to get up from their afternoon naps to say hello to a stranger.

"Rome is at the branding corral," Casey said. "There's no road so you'll have to ride."

Cloe couldn't remember the last time she'd ridden. Daddy had sold the horses more than a year ago and Brandon had never been a horse lover so they hadn't ever gone riding. But as soon as she mounted the pretty filly Casey saddled for her, it felt like coming home. Tears welled in her eyes. Something Casey didn't miss.

"You okay?" he asked.

"It's just been a while. I didn't realize how much I missed it."

He nodded. "Once a ranch kid, always a ranch kid." He pointed to the open land behind the stables. "The branding corral is just about three miles that way. Keep heading west and you'll see it on your right. Since it's been a while, I'd take it slow until you feel comfortable in the saddle again."

Cloe agreed, but the spirited filly wanted no part of walking at a sedate pace. As soon as Cloe got past the stables, the horse started tugging at the reins and prancing fitfully. Cloe kept a firm seat and waited for the horse to settle down before she nudged her into a walk. After a while, she took her into a trot before she gave the horse free rein.

The filly took off and it was sheer heaven. The cold wind pulled her hair from the clip and whipped it around as the bright Texas sun kissed her face and glistened off the horse's chestnut coat. In the air there was a hint of spring and beneath her the muscles of the horse flexed and stretched as they raced over the grazing land. She would have raced right past the corral if a shrill whistle hadn't caused the horse to slow and change directions.

The branding corral was a confusion of cowboys on horseback and cattle, but it wasn't hard to figure out who had whistled when the horse trotted right up to the cowboy who had just, effortlessly, swung over the corral railing.

Rome was dusty from head to toe. Even though it was cold, he wore only a flannel shirt with a light blue Henley beneath that made his eyes appear the color of a robin's egg when his gaze met hers. There was confusion in them and she suddenly felt stupid for riding all the way out there and taking him away from his work.

"I'm sorry," she said. "I shouldn't bother you while you're busy. I can come back later."

He shook his head. "No. I'm glad you came." He pulled off his hat and wiped the sweat from his brow as he called back to the cowboys working in the corral. "I'll be back in a few."

There was a chorus of "'Kay, boss." and "Sure thing, boss." Then before Cloe realized what was happening, Rome moved her foot out of the stirrup and replaced it with his before he swung up behind her. His arms encircled her waist, but he didn't try to take the reins.

"Head over to those trees."

She guided the horse to the copse of mesquite and oak trees, trying to ignore the scent of hardworking man and the press of Rome's hot, hard body. It was impossible. Her heart seemed to be beating out of her chest and it was a struggle to breathe.

It was a relief when they reached the trees and he swung down. He reached up to help her dismount. When she was on the ground, he smiled.

"I see you didn't forget how to ride in the big city."

She patted the horse's neck. "No, and I missed it."

"I could tell. You looked like you could have ridden all the way to Mexico if I hadn't whistled."

She smiled. "We used to have a horse I taught to come when I whistled because I couldn't say his name."

His eyes squinted. "Why couldn't you say his name?"

She stroked the horse's silky forehead. "I had a stutter when I was a little kid. I struggled with my d's and the horse's name was Dandy."

"You stuttered? I don't remember that."

"I was extremely good at masking it. I either avoided all words I couldn't say or I just didn't say anything."

His gray eyes stared back at her from the shadow of his hat. "So that's why you were so quiet. Although it doesn't explain why you still are."

"Habit."

He nodded. "Those are hard to break."

"And what are your habits?"

He took off his hat and slapped at his jeans, causing plumes of dust to rise. "Working too much." He put his hat back on. "So what brings you to the Remington Ranch, Lucky?"

"Lucky?"

He grinned. "Since your name is Clover, I figured it was a suitable nickname."

"Well, you figured wrong. I'm about as unlucky as a person can get. I never win anything."

"Maybe nicknaming you Lucky will change that."

She laughed. "Doubtful. And the reason I'm here is to apologize for what my grandmother said to you last night about marrying one of her granddaughters."

"Not one," he said. "You."

Her cheeks heated. "I'm sorry. Finding out we spent the night together in the hayloft and that you and I have become . . . friends has made her think her ridiculous plan just might work. Now she refuses to sell the ranch. And I can't make her realize that if she doesn't sell, she'll lose it anyway."

Rome didn't seem surprised. "Who is this loan shark your grandmother mentioned last night?"

So her grandmother had told Rome more than she should have. "They aren't loan sharks. It's an investment company, Oleander Investments, that helped Daddy consolidate all his real estate contracts with a loan."

"How many payments has your father missed?"

"A lot."

"So they could foreclose?"

Cloe nodded. "And no doubt they will if we don't come up with the money. I was hoping we could just sell the land and keep the house. But the loan is too big. We'll need to sell the land and the house to even come close to paying it off. Of course, that's a moot point because Mimi refuses to sell. She doesn't seem to realize that we don't have a choice. Sell or get kicked out. And being kicked off our beloved ranch will not only be humiliating to my family, but also heartbreaking."

There was a long stretch of silence and Cloe realized she'd said too much. She didn't need to burden him with her problems. "I'm sorry. With my sisters gone, I just needed to talk to someone about it."

"You don't need to apologize." He hesitated. "I'm not going to lie, Cloe. I've been giving a lot of thought to buying the ranch since you asked me if I was interested in it. I'd like to buy it. If we can talk Mimi into selling to me, I'll pay off the loan and let your family keep their house and the land it sits on."

She blinked. "You would?" He nodded and a

small flicker of hope came to life before it was snuffed out. "It wouldn't matter. She doesn't want the land belonging to anyone but family."

He studied her for a long moment before he spoke. "Then we'll just have to give her what she wants . . . or make her think we are."

"What do you mean?"

His smoky-gray gaze was direct. "You want to get married, Lucky?"

CHAPTER NINE

EVEN THOUGH HE looked serious, Cloe knew he had to be joking. But since wedding proposals were a touchy subject, she couldn't find the humor in it. "Don't joke, Rome. It's not funny."

"I'm not joking." As she stared at him with stunned shock, he continued. "I want your land. I was planning on making your father an offer as soon as the house went up for sale."

"But you know he would never sell to a Remington."

"I thought I could change his mind." He hesitated. "With your help."

The pieces of the puzzle she hadn't been able to fit together suddenly fell into place. No wonder Rome was being so nice to her. He was interested in buying Holiday Ranch and he thought starting a friendship up with her would help his cause. She should have pieced things together sooner and realized his attention had nothing to do with her and everything to do with the ranch.

She felt more than a little stupid . . . and hurt.

Something her face must have shown.

"It's not what you're thinking, Cloe," he said. "I've enjoyed hanging out with you."

She forced a smile. "Of course you have. Everyone knows I'm a barrel of laughs. And there's no need to lie, Rome. I'm sure you got the idea of charming a Holiday sister to get the ranch from my grandmother when she offered us up like prime cuts of meat. You thought why not choose the least attractive sister? The one most likely to succumb to Remington charm."

He flinched. "It wasn't like that. Yes, I'll admit I was hoping you'd give me information about the house going up for sale and possibly put a good word in with your daddy, but I'm not lying about enjoying our time together. I never realized how much we have in common. We both feel responsible for our siblings, we both have stubborn daddies, and we both got our hearts broken."

"And our commonalities are reason enough to marry me?"

"No. But it looks like it's the only way to get what we both want. You want your family to be able to keep their home. I want your land."

"And you're willing to marry a woman you don't love for it? Did you get a concussion when you fell off my grandmother's trellis? Because you must have some kind of brain damage to think I'd agreed to marry a man who only wanted to be my friend to get a piece of land." She knew her temper was showing, but she didn't care anymore. The man was unbelievable. "I wouldn't marry you if you were the last man on earth."

Instead of looking upset, he laughed. "There's that redheaded temper you hide so well."

Her eyes widened and her voice rose. "I do not have a temper or red hair! And this entire situation is no laughing matter."

His smile faded. "You're right. It isn't funny. I wish I could just pay off your debt, Mimi would sign me over the land, and your family could keep their home. That would be the best thing for everyone. But stubborn people aren't always smart. Believe me, I know. My daddy has made some pretty stupid choices based on his strong beliefs about family heritage and the sanctity of the land. And, in order to keep our ranch successful and thriving, I've had to learn ways around his stubbornness. Yes, I've had to be a little deceitful. But sometimes you have to hide the truth for the greater good. Mimi and your family will lose everything if we don't make her think she got her way. Not to mention that the Holiday Ranch has some prime grazing land and water. Acquiring it would make Remington Ranch one of the biggest ranches in Texas. And yeah, I'm egotistical enough to like the thought of that. I also like the thought of having my own land to do with what I want without my father putting in his two cents."

"You want the land enough to marry me for it? I thought you never wanted to get married again."

"I don't. But this wouldn't be a real marriage."

She stared at him. "What do you mean? You want to pretend we're married when we're not?"

"I wish it was that easy. But I think your grandmother is too smart for that. I think she'll want proof before she signs over anything. No, we'll have to get married. But she didn't say we had to stay married."

Cloe couldn't believe what she was hearing. "So we'll get married and then quickly divorce?"

"Not quickly or everyone will know it was all fake. I don't think it's a good idea for anyone to know about our plan."

"You want us to lie to everyone? Our families, friends, the townsfolk?"

He lifted his eyebrows. "You think your parents and sisters would let you go through with it if they found out? I know my brother and daddy sure wouldn't—even if they'll all benefit from it."

She didn't know what to say. "But it's crazy . . . it's just plain crazy."

He sighed heavily and ran a hand over his face. "You're right. I don't know what I was thinking. Maybe I did suffer a little brain damage in the fall." He looked at her. "Come on. I'll take you back to your car."

He helped her mount and then got on behind her. This time, he held the reins, his arms encircling her in hard muscle and radiant heat. But between her anger at him only befriending her to get the ranch and his offer of marriage, her thoughts were too jumbled to notice.

A fake marriage? What was he thinking? There was no way she was going to marry a man she didn't love. Especially a man who had only been nice to her to get her family's land. She didn't know who she was maddest at. Rome or herself for being so gullible.

They rode in silence all the way back to the ranch. When they got there, Rome swung down and then held out a hand for her. She ignored it and dismounted on her own. Once on the ground, she stroked the horse's forehead and patted her withers.

"Thanks for the ride, beautiful girl."

"Lady Grantham."

Cloe glanced at Rome, and he shrugged. "Casey named her. He has a thing for *Downton Abbey*. We also have a goat named Mister Carson and a milk cow named Daisy Mason. He wanted to name the last mare we bought Lady Mary, but I figured one lady was enough."

She might have laughed if she hadn't felt so upset. "Tell Casey thanks for letting me ride her."

"You're welcome to come riding anytime." When she didn't say anything, he stepped closer. "Look, Cloe, I know you're mad at me, but I really would like to be your friend. Tomorrow night is Twofer Margarita Night at the Hellhole. Why don't you meet me and I'll get you that margarita you've been craving. I'll even pick you up so you don't have to be the designated driver."

"No, thank you. I'm not craving margaritas." Or arrogant cowboys. She turned to leave, but he stopped her.

"Come on, Lucky. Give me another chance."

She spoke without turning around. "Cloe. Only friends and family have the right to give people nicknames."

When she reached her car, Casey came out of the house. He seemed as good at reading her moods as Rome was. "So I guess you found my brother. Just like our daddy, he excels at running women off."

"Thank you for letting me ride Lady Grantham."

He nodded. "Anytime." She opened her car door, but before she could get in, he stopped her. "Don't give up on him, Cloe. He might be inept with women, but he really is a good man."

A good man, my foot, she thought as she backed out and drove away from Remington Ranch.

By the time she got to the house, the sun was setting. Its tangerine rays spread around the two-story farmhouse like the marmalade jam her mama canned every summer. The orange sunset highlighted the soft green the house had been painted. Mama had spent hours picking out the color from the samples she brought home from the hardware store. She said it reminded her of her family's eyes when they were happy and content.

Cloe wasn't happy and content now. She was angry and hurt. She didn't know why. She hadn't even given Rome one thought before Sweetie and Decker's wedding and now suddenly she felt like she'd lost her best friend. It was foolish. They weren't friends and they never would be.

Another foolish thing was putting up with her grandmother's stubbornness. Mimi needed to accept that the ranch had to be sold. Climbing the porch steps, she mentally prepared herself for battle with her grandmother. At the door, she took a deep breath before reaching for the screen door handle.

"Bad news?"

She lowered her hand and turned to see her mama sitting on the porch swing. With her thick black hair and green eyes, Darla Holiday was an extremely attractive woman. Petite and energetic, she had always reminded Cloe of a bumblebee— always working and never sitting still for long. Of course, with six daughters and a demanding husband, you had to have energy just to keep up.

But she seemed to be still now.

"Hey, Mama. What are you doing out here in the cold?"

"Just enjoying the sunset." She opened the throw blanket she had wrapped around her and patted the swing next to her. "Come join me." As soon as Cloe sat down, her mama pulled her close and wrapped the blanket around her. "So what's the bad news? And don't tell me that there isn't any. You look like you're carrying the weight of the world on your shoulders."

"I'm worried we're not going to be able to talk Mimi into selling the ranch. She just can't seem to realize that the ranch will be foreclosed on if she doesn't."

Her mother's chest rose as she took a deep breath and slowly released it. "I think she's holding out for a miracle."

"Or one of her granddaughters to marry a Remington."

Mama hesitated. "I noticed the broken trellis and Mimi told me what happened. Is there something going on with you and Rome?"

Anger reared its ugly head again. "Nothing. He was just interested in buying the ranch and thought I could help him convince Daddy to sell to him."

"Ahh. That's too bad."

Cloe sat up and looked at her mother with disbelief. "Don't tell me that you were hoping I'd get with Rome too. I just broke up with Brandon."

Her mother shrugged. "I've always liked Rome. And just because you broke things off with Brandon, that doesn't mean you can't find love again. I did."

Cloe stared at her. "You were in love before Daddy?"

"I was. I fell in love in high school. At least, I thought it was love. But I discovered the difference when I met your daddy."

"Was it love at first sight?"

Mama huffed. "Young people today. Y'all think everything should happen in a blink of an eye. I didn't love your father at first sight. In fact, I'd known him for years and never once even considered him as a boyfriend. But then he came into Crawley's General Store one day when I was working. It was right after I'd broken up with my boyfriend. We started talking and discovered we had a lot of the same values and beliefs. But it wasn't until he brought me here to the ranch and I met his family that I started thinking of him as more than just a friend. When I saw your father in his element that was when I saw the real Hank Holiday." She smiled softly as she stared off. "Lord, he loves this ranch. I don't know how he'll survive losing it. Or Mimi for that matter."

Or you. Cloe thought as she studied her mama's sad face. But Darla Holiday had never been one to wallow too long in self-pity. She shook her head and got up from the swing.

"Enough dawdling. I have supper to make." She leaned down and took Cloe's cheeks in her cold hands and gave her a determined look. "You will love again, Clover Fields Holiday. All you have to do is keep your heart open." She kissed her forehead before she released her. "Now let's go in. It's much too cold to be out here."

Cloe shook her head. "You go on in, Mama. I'll be in to help with supper in a few minutes."

Mama studied her and sighed. "You always have been my responsible baby. The one who felt like you had to watch out for everyone else. But, honey, you don't need to carry the weight of this family on your shoulders. No matter what happens to this ranch, me, your daddy, and Mimi will be just fine. You'll see."

Once her mother had gone back inside, Cloe wrapped up in the blanket and stared out at the fast-growing darkness. She wished she could believe everything her mother had said. She wished she would find love again. And she wished no matter what happened with the ranch that her family would be just fine. But she knew in her heart the chances of those things happening were slim to none.

As she sat there in the porch swing her grand-father had made for Mimi on their first wedding anniversary, she realized she could live without finding love. What she couldn't live with was having a way to keep this ranch for her family and not taking it.

CHAPTER TEN

ROME HAD BEEN more than a little surprised when he'd gotten the text from Cloe saying she'd meet him at the Hellhole tonight. He thought for sure she'd never talk to him again. The look in her eyes when she had figured out he had been using their friendship to get the ranch had made him feel like he'd been mule-kicked in the stomach.

Maybe that was why he'd come up with his harebrained idea of marriage. He'd wanted to remove that look of hurt and disappointment from her green eyes. He'd wanted to prove he wasn't a lowdown snake in the grass by offering her family a way out of their problems. At that point, he hadn't even cared about the land. He'd just wanted to see her eyes sparkle and her dimples flash.

Instead, she had looked at him as if he'd lost his mind.

He had.

Marry Cloe?

What a ridiculous idea. Getting married was

the last thing he wanted to do. Even if it wouldn't be real.

"Hey, Rome."

He stopped searching the bar for Cloe and turned to see Sissy Haskins standing there. Sissy ran the beauty salon in town and was one of the women Rome had hooked up with after getting his heart smashed to smithereens by Emily. He'd made it clear he wasn't interested in a repeat. Sissy had yet to get the message.

She smiled at him with a look that said she was more than available. "You want to buy a girl a drink?"

Never one to refuse a woman a drink, he motioned for the waitress then pointed at Sissy. But when Sissy hooked an arm through his and started pulling him toward the bar, he shook his head. "Sorry, Sis, but I'm meeting someone."

She drew back. "Who? Casey? I'm sure he won't mind if I join y'all."

"Actually, it's not Casey. It's a friend." He knew by the ticked-off look on her face that she didn't believe it was just a friend. She released his arm. "So who is the lucky girl who has finally gotten you over your ex-wife?"

About then, his gaze landed on Cloe sitting at a back table. Her hair was in one of those twisty buns and her hands were primly folded on the table in front of her. She looked nervous. The heels of her cowboy boots bounced up and down on the rung of the stool her toes rested on.

"Cloe Holiday?" Sissy said.

Rather than explain, he just shot Sissy a smile. "Enjoy your drink, Sis."

Without saying another word, he headed toward the table where Cloe sat. She looked up as he approached. Her green eyes stared back at him through the lenses of her glasses. Unlike Sissy, there was no brown shadow on her eyelids, no dark eyeliner rimming her eyes, no fake-looking lashes curling almost to her eyebrows, or sticky-looking gloss on her lips.

She just looked fresh and natural.

"I thought you weren't coming," she said.

"I had to stop for gas." He took his hat off before he sat down on the stool across from her. "And just so you know, when I say I'm going to meet someone, I meet them." He glanced at the water in the glass in front of her. "I thought you wanted to try a margarita."

"I need to keep a clear head."

"Your sisters aren't here, Cloe. I'll drive you home if you have too much to drink."

She shifted in the chair and he knew she was bouncing her heels again. "It's not that. I need to keep a clear head for our discussion."

"Our discussion about what? If this has to do with me trying to get the ranch by befriending you, I'm sorry. I mean it."

"That's not what I came here to talk to you about." She cleared her throat. "I've thought about your offer and I'm willing to accept."

He stared at her. "My offer? What—" He cut off when he realized what she was talking about.

His eyes widened and before he could get any words out, she continued in a rush.

"I know I said it was crazy—and it is. But so is losing a house that my family built and have always called home. You're right. Sometimes you have to be a little deceitful for the better good." She opened her purse and pulled out a folded piece of paper. Her hands shook as she smoothed it out on the table. "I thought it would be best if everything was written out in black and white." She stared down at the list with the neat handwriting. "Although I guess I used a blue pen—anyway, the first thing is that we don't tell anyone. Not even our siblings. Although I think my sisters will probably be able to figure it out, but by that time it will be too late for them to do anything about it. Which brings us to the next point. We need to get married right away. Not only because the loan needs to be paid off, but also because I'm horrible at keeping secrets. Third—"

Rome finally found his voice. "Whoa there. I know this was my plan, but you were right. It is crazy."

She blinked. "So you don't want to marry me?"

Why did she sound hurt? "Uhh . . . well, it's not that I don't want to marry you. I don't want to marry anyone."

"But, like you said, it won't be a real marriage. It will be fake." She pointed down at the paper. "That's point number three. We'll only stay married a few months before we say that we're just not compatible and get a divorce. It will be believable because . . ." She hesitated and he finished for her.

"Because that's exactly what happened with Emily and folks will just think the Remingtons struggle to hold onto their wives."

She shook her head. "That's not what I was going to say at all. I was going to say it will be believable because no one will think we make a good couple."

"Why is that?"

"Because you could get any woman you wanted. Why settle for me?"

He squinted at her. "You know I'm getting a little sick and tired of you putting yourself down, Luck—Cloe. You'd make a damn fine wife. You're practical, smart, kind, and hardworking."

She laughed. "You sound like my sister. And like I told her, those traits aren't top of every man's wife-hunting list."

"Well, if they aren't, they should be."

"So you'll marry me."

"No."

She scrunched her nose to push her glasses back up. "But it was your idea. And it's a good one. You'll get the land you covet and my family won't have to move out of the house they love." She paused. "And my daddy would be happy to help you out whenever you need an extra ranch hand."

He knew what she was wanting. She wanted her father to still feel like he was useful to the ranch. He could understand that. He'd be lost if he didn't have a ranch to work. "I'd have no problem with Hank still working the ranch. But I just don't think—"

She cut him off. "I'm a good cook. While I'm living with you, I'll cook for you and your brother and your daddy. My mama taught me how to make pot roast, chicken potpie, chicken and dumplings, braised short ribs, Texas chocolate sheet cake, and blackberry pie."

His stomach rumbled. "Blackberry pie?" He had tasted Darla's blackberry pie. It was the best thing he'd ever put in his mouth. He shook himself out of his food trance. "It won't work."

"Why?"

Deep down, he knew why. He just couldn't say.

But when he didn't say anything, Cloe figured it out. "You're afraid that the wallflower is going to get too attached to you."

He sighed. "I don't want you to get hurt. I'm not someone who can make any woman happy, Cloe."

"After Brandon, believe me when I tell you that I'm not looking for a man to make me happy. This is strictly a business proposition. We're going to be business partners. Once our business is concluded, there will be no need for us to ever speak again."

The thought of never speaking to her again bothered him. It bothered him a lot.

The waitress arrived to take his order. He usually ordered a beer, but tonight he needed something a little stronger. He ordered a double shot of whiskey for himself and two margaritas for Cloe. When the waitress left, he shrugged.

"There's nothing clearheaded about what we're thinking about doing so I figure we might as well drink."

She didn't argue. In fact, when their drinks came, she took a big slug of her margarita. The sight of the light green frothy mustache on her top lip made him smile.

"So what do you think?" he asked.

"I now understand why my sisters love them." She licked the froth off, and watching her pink tongue slide over her lip caused a stab of heat to slice through him. He jerked his gaze away and took a swallow of his own drink. Once the burn of liquor had doused that heat, he looked back at her.

"So are we really doing this?"

She stared at him with eyes that held determination and fear. "It's the only way we can both get what we want."

He couldn't deny he wanted Holiday Ranch. Running his own ranch had become an all-consuming dream. But something else pushed him to lift his glass. Something he couldn't define. "Then I guess we're getting married."

She lifted her glass and clinked it against his before they both took a sip. An awkward silence followed. She carefully folded the piece of paper and put it back in her purse before she spoke.

"I don't mind cooking, but I refuse to iron. I had to press my daddy's shirts when I was a kid and swore I would never iron again." She looked at his almost-empty glass. "How much do you drink?"

"I have the occasional beer and whiskey, but I'm not an alcoholic, if that's what you're asking."

"Do all alcoholics know they're alcoholics?"

He grinned. "Point taken. But you can ask Casey. He thinks I'm a teetotaler. Of course, he's a partier. I've had to get him out of more scrapes than I can count because he's had one too many."

She nodded. "I know how that goes. Growing up, I was always covering for my sisters so they wouldn't get in trouble with our daddy."

"And they never had to cover for you?"

"Getting into trouble isn't in my nature."

"Trouble doesn't have to be in your nature to get into it. You just have to be willing." He waggled his eyebrows. "Or have a good instigator."

The dimples appeared and he felt like doing a cartwheel. "I had five instigators, but someone has to be the voice of reason. Of course, I'm not really being the voice of reason now."

That said a lot. Cloe wasn't just her sisters' keeper, but also their conscience. It was quite a burden to carry. "No wonder you felt like you had to hide in the hayloft just to cut loose a little."

Her eyes flashed with anger. He realized he liked seeing her temper as much as he liked seeing her smile. "I wasn't hiding in the hayloft. I just needed a moment to myself."

He lifted his eyebrows. "You took more than a moment, Cloe."

"Because I made the mistake of getting drunk and I didn't want to make a scene and embarrass my family."

"But isn't that what weddings are for? Everyone

drinks a little too much and does embarrassing things. Casey and Noelle got drunk and knocked over the wedding cake." That was the commotion he and Belle had heard the night of the wedding. Casey had laughed himself silly when he'd told Rome. Of course, he hadn't thought knocking the cake over was as funny as Noelle being covered in cake and icing.

"But that's different," Cloe said.

"Why? Why is it okay for your sisters to cut loose and it's not okay for you to?"

It was obvious she was getting frustrated with his line of questioning. Her forehead was knitted above her glasses and her lips were pressed in a firm line. "It has nothing to do with whether it's okay or not. Maybe I just don't like cutting loose."

"And maybe you just haven't had the right person to cut loose with." He got up and held out his hand. "Dance with me."

She shook her head. "I told you before, I don't dance."

"And I don't believe you. I've seen teen movies. I know girls love to dance around their rooms in their underwear singing into hairbrushes."

"I have never sung into a hairbrush."

He cocked his head. "Does that mean you have danced around in your underwear?" When she refused to answer, he laughed. "I knew it! Teen movies don't lie. Now come on, Cloe. If people see us dancing, they'll be more likely to believe in our hoax." He grinned. "And I promise you can keep your clothes on."

A hint of a smile tipped the corners of her mouth and he knew he had her. Why that made him feel like punching the air and crowing, he didn't know.

"Fine," she said. "But only one dance. And don't complain if your toes get crushed."

All eyes were on them when he led her through the bar to the dance floor. He could read the surprise and curiosity on the townsfolk's faces. He understood. Until recently, he had never considered dating Cloe Holiday and would have been surprised if someone had suggested it. Not only because their daddies were feuding, but also because she hadn't even been on his radar. Now he was considering marrying her. Correction, he was marrying her. They'd clinked glasses on it. That was as good as a handshake.

He should feel scared about getting married again. He didn't. He was going into this marriage with his eyes wide open and his heart not attached. He felt like he did when he purchased a fine piece of horseflesh—secure in the knowledge that he had made a good decision.

Once on the dance floor, he drew her into his arms. He liked that she was tall enough to look him in the eyes. Her waist was whipcord thin and her hand felt soft and cool in his. It trembled.

"Hey." He gave her hand a gentle squeeze. "This is no big deal. It's just a couple quick steps and a couple slow."

It turned out Cloe *had* danced with her sisters. Either that or she was just a natural. It only took one lap around the dance floor for her steps to fall into synch with his. On the fourth lap, he tried twirling her under his arm. She missed a step but then quickly got it back. By the time the song ended, she had the two-step down cold. When the next song started, she didn't offer any resistance when he continued to dance her around the floor.

He knew she was enjoying herself. He knew from the twinkle in her green eyes and the flush of her cheeks and the continual appearance of her dimples. And surprisingly, he was enjoying himself too. They two-stepped for three songs straight before the band switched to a slow waltz. Cloe mastered that as easily as she'd mastered the two-step. He was the one who struggled when her breasts pressed against his chest.

He tried to keep his thoughts from the tempting pillows melting into his pecs. "So you lied. You did dance around in your underwear."

A teeth-flashing, dimple-popping smile broke over her face. Rome felt like he'd been sucker punched hard in the chest. The brilliance of her smile knocked the wind right out of him.

"Okay, so I danced with my sisters. But not in my underwear. In pajamas."

He liked the image of her dancing and laughing with her sisters. He wanted to hear her laugh. But for now, he just wanted to keep the breathtaking smile on her face.

He twirled her under his arm and then dipped her.

"Rome!" she squealed.

"Don't worry. I got you." He lifted her back to

her feet and continued to dance her around the floor until her cellphone pinged.

She stopped dancing and pulled it from her back pocket to read the text. "I need to go. My mama's worried. I completely blindsided her when I told her I was coming to the Hellhole tonight. I'm not a bar person."

"You didn't tell her you were meeting me?"

"I didn't want Mimi getting too excited if things didn't work out. She's going to be overjoyed that her plan succeeded."

As he looked into Cloe's green eyes, Rome felt pretty overjoyed himself. "I'll walk you out."

He hadn't realized he'd parked right next to Cloe's car until she stopped at the Honda Civic. The sight of the small white car sitting next to his big black truck made him smile. "Darth Vader and Princess Leia." He thought he would have to explain, but she came right back.

"Voldemort and Hermione."

He sent her a wounded look. "Voldemort? At least, Darth had a good heart underneath his villainous exterior. How about Daffy Duck and Snoopy?"

Her eyes crinkled behind the lenses of her glasses. "But they don't go together."

"Yes, they do. They're both beloved cartoon friends."

"They aren't friends. They don't even know each other."

"I bet if they met, they'd hit it off."

"A duck and a beagle?"

"Why not?" He grinned. "A Remington and a Holiday are becoming friends."

"And soon-to-be husband and wife." She shook her head. "This is crazy."

"Maybe. But maybe it's time we were the wild and crazy ones of the family."

She must have liked the thought because the breathtaking smile came back. He didn't know what happened. One second, he was standing there looking at those smiling lips and the next second he was taking her chin in his hand and brushing his lips over hers. It was just a simple kiss, just something to seal their deal. But there was nothing simple about his reaction. Just the touch of her soft lips had desire washing over him like slow-rolling waves.

She tasted like he thought clouds would taste— soft and sweet—and he couldn't resist deepening the kiss. His hand dropped from her chin and settled on her waist, drawing her closer. Her hands lifted to his shoulders and her lips slid open, offering him the wet heat of her mouth. When he hesitantly dipped his tongue inside, her tongue was there to greet it, making him lose all thoughts of soft and sweet.

He stepped her back against her car and fed on her lips like a starving man—sucking, nipping, stroking—as his hands slipped beneath her loose sweater and wandered over the warm, naked skin of her back. When his fingertips brushed the hooks of her bra, all he could think about was unfastening those hooks and filling his hands with her lush breasts.

But before he could, Cloe pushed him away. Her eyes were wide and confused. "Why did you do that?"

He didn't have an answer. He felt as stunned as she looked. Why *had* he kissed her? And why did he feel like he'd just been struck by lightning? While he was struggling to get his emotions under control, Cloe glanced over his shoulder.

"Oh. I get it. Melba Wadley is standing over there watching us."

Since he was still feeling blindsided, he latched on to the excuse. "Yeah . . . uhh . . . Melba. Since she's a friend of Mimi's, I figured her seeing us kissing would help convince your grandmother our marriage is real."

She pressed her lips together and nodded. "Of course. And speaking of our marriage, we should probably decide when and where. I was thinking next week in College Station. The mother of one of my students works at the courthouse and I'm sure she can get us a license and also make an appointment with a judge."

It was amazing how calm she was. Like they were making a date for lunch. He didn't feel calm. Not after that kiss. But he tried to act like he was. "Sounds good. Just let me know what time. You can text me."

She hesitated as if she wanted to say something, but then she only lifted a hand before she got in her car.

He was standing there watching her pull away when Melba stepped up.

Melba worked at the sheriff office with Decker.

She managed the office and dealt with all the incoming calls and decided who actually needed law enforcement and who was just calling to complain. She also fostered animals she was always trying to pawn off on him.

Tonight was no different.

She opened the purse she had slung across her body and drew out a tiny tiger-striped kitten. "I wanted to introduce you to Taylor Swift." Melba named all the animals she fostered after country singers. Which made it that much harder for the people of Wilder to refuse them. Rome included.

"Sorry, Mel, but Tammy, Waylon, Reba, Blake, and George Jones don't need another friend. And just so you know, Taylor hasn't sung country for years."

Melba lifted her chin haughtily. "Once country always country." She glanced at the empty spot where Cloe's car had been parked. "And that doesn't just apply to singers. Cloe Holiday is a country girl who belongs right here in Wilder." She winked at him. "And there's nothing like a handsome cowboy to make her realize that."

Rome winked back. "Then maybe I'll just have to marry the girl."

CHAPTER ELEVEN

A MARCH WINTER STORM hit on Cloe's wedding day. She had picked out her nicest dress to wear, but it seemed impractical with the frigid temperature and icy rain. So when she arrived at the Remington Ranch, she was bundled up in her warmest coat, a knit hat, a turtleneck sweater, jeans, and her furry boots.

Being that she was so early, she thought she'd have to knock on the door. But Rome was waiting for her on the porch with his black Stetson pulled low and the collar of his sheepskin jacket flipped up around his clean-shaven jaw.

He didn't waste time helping her out of the car and into his truck. Once he was in the driver's side, he took off his hat and set it on the console. She thought he would look as nervous as she felt. She should have known better. Rome wasn't the nervous type. Of course, she didn't think he'd look so happy either. His smile was bright and his eyes twinkled with humor.

"Perfect day for a wedding."

She shivered. "If you're a polar bear."

He reached over and pushed her glasses up

before he tapped the end of her cold nose with his warm finger. "I promise I'll buy you some hot chocolate after, Lucky."

She thought the drive to College Station would be awkward, but they talked the entire way about people they remembered from school and the latest gossip going around town. Before she knew it they were parking at the courthouse.

"Did you bring the wedding license?" he asked.

She nodded and pulled it out of her purse, along with the prenuptial agreement he had given her and she had signed. She didn't blame him for wanting to make sure she didn't get any part of his family's ranch after they divorced. He was already more than generous by bailing her family out of debt and allowing them to keep their home.

The judge who married them was a solemn woman who didn't waste any time on pleasantries.

"You can hang your coats on the rack right over there in the corner and then we'll get started."

Rome helped Cloe off with her coat and hung it on the rack before he took off his. To her embarrassment, underneath his sheepskin coat he wore a nice jacket, dress shirt, and tie. She wished she hadn't been so practical and had worn the dress she picked out. She also wished she had skipped the knit hat. Static electricity crackled when she pulled it off and she knew her hair stood on end. She quickly tried to smooth it and caught Rome watching her.

"You left it down."

She tried to bring some order to the wild curls. "I probably shouldn't have."

He shook his head. "No. I like it down. You have pretty hair."

Before she could get over the compliment, he took her hand and led her over to where the judge and her assistant were waiting.

The ceremony was short, but it felt like it lasted a lifetime. Her hand Rome held was sweating like a cold glass of iced tea in late August and her heart was thumping out of control. By the time it was her turn to speak, she reverted back to her stuttering.

"I d-d-do."

Rome's voice, on the other hand, was strong and clear. "I do."

When the judge pronounced them man and wife, she didn't say "You may kiss the bride." But Rome did anyway. It was nothing like the kiss he had given her in the Hellhole's parking lot. She didn't feel like she'd been sucked into the center of the sun and was burning from the inside out. This kiss was brief, just a slight brush of lips. Still, it left her feeling dazed. Or maybe she was dazed about the entire situation.

She was married.

To Rome Remington.

If someone had asked her the least likely person she'd marry, Rome's name would have been on the list. In the elevator, she stood next to Rome and stared at their reflections in the metal doors. They looked like the odd couple they were. Tall,

handsome husband and his dowdy, dazed-look-
ing wife.

After leaving the courthouse, Rome asked
about a good place to get lunch. Even though she
wasn't hungry, Cloe suggested her favorite coffee
shop that served the best paninis. Unfortunately,
she didn't even think about it being Brandon's
favorite place too. Rome had just brought their
order to the table when Brandon walked in the
door with Sabrina Hayes, a third-grade teacher
who worked at the same school as Cloe and
Brandon. They were holding hands and laughing
as they brushed ice off each other's coats.

Cloe just froze. She couldn't look away. She
couldn't dive under the table. She couldn't do
anything but sit there feeling like she'd just been
slapped hard in the face.

"Cloe?" Rome said. "What's wrong?" He
turned to follow her gaze and must have put two
and two together. When he turned back around,
his eyes held concern and compassion. "Is that
Brandon?"

She nodded and was finally able to pull her
gaze away. "I want to go."

He didn't argue or mention their untouched
sandwiches. He just pushed back his chair and
pulled on his coat before helping her on with
hers. She clung tightly to his arm and kept her
head down, hoping they could get out the door
without being seen.

That wasn't the case.

"Cloe?"

It was Sabrina who had spoken. Cloe wanted to

ignore her and keep walking, but Rome stopped, forcing her to stop too.

Sabrina stood with Brandon at the order counter. Brandon must not have seen Cloe until that moment because he looked stunned . . . and then embarrassed. He quickly released Sabrina's hand and stepped away.

"Uhh . . . Cloe. What are you doing here? I thought you were in Wilder with your family."

It took every speech technique she'd ever learned to hide the turmoil inside her and speak normally. "I just came into town for the day. What are you doing here on a school day?"

"School was closed because of the bad weather." Brandon glanced at Rome and Rome held out a hand.

"Rome Remington. Cloe's husband."

Cloe cringed as Brandon's eyes widened. "Husband?" He looked at her for verification. As she struggled to find words, Rome sent her a teasing smile.

"You didn't tell your friends about us gettin' married, honey?" He looked back at Brandon. "We've known each other since grade school. Of course, life takes you down different paths. I went to one college and she went to another. But when she showed up in town a couple months ago, all I can say is that the sparks flew." He winked. "If you know what I mean."

Brandon stared at Rome in stunned horror before he turned to Cloe. "A couple months ago? We were still living together a couple months ago."

Rome playfully socked him in the arm. Although from Brandon's cringe it wasn't so playfully. "Sorry, dude, but love just happens."

Brandon rubbed his arm and looked back at Cloe with accusation in his eyes. "Well, it's a good thing I figured out you weren't the right woman for me."

His words jolted Cloe out of the hurt she'd been feeling and anger sizzled through her veins. "Hallie was right all along," she said. "You are a selfish, arrogant asshole." She looked at Rome. "Can you wait one second, honey. I'm going to get a to-go box. I think I'm hungry after all."

She was still seething when they were back in Rome's truck. "The absolute gall of the man! He condemned me when he was obviously the one who has been fooling around behind my back with Sabrina Hayes. And I should have known. I can't tell you how many times I caught them giggling in the teachers' lounge, but like an idiot I just stuck my head in the sand and convinced myself that Brandon would never cheat on me. How wrong I was!"

"Maybe he didn't cheat while you were dating."

She turned on him. "Don't you dare defend him! He cheated all right. If not physically, mentally."

Rome held up his hands. "Hey, don't yell at me. I'm just an innocent bystander."

"Who told him we were married."

"We are." He grinned as he started the truck.

"And did you see the look on his face? I swear his jaw dropped clean down to his chest."

She still felt hurt. And betrayed. And mad as hell. But she also felt . . . like she had just smashed Brandon in the face with the cream pie of justice. There was only one person she had to thank for that. If Rome hadn't been there, she would have walked out without saying anything. It was Rome who made her stop. Rome who handed her the cream pie.

She looked at him. "Thank you."

He winked. "What are husbands for?"

By the time they got back to the Remington Ranch, the icy rain had stopped, but it was still freezing cold. They planned to break the news to his brother and father first. Then head over to the Holiday Ranch to tell her family.

Cloe didn't look forward to doing either. She was a nervous wreck when she stepped into Rome's house.

"It's going to be fine," Rome said as he helped her off with her coat. "Casey likes you and my daddy has been bugging me to get married ever since Emily left."

"Not to a Holiday."

He hung their coats on a rack by the door. "That might be a little surprising, but he'll get over it."

They found Sam sitting in his study reading a book. The room was far cozier than the rest of the house with its paneled walls, western art, and the fire blazing in the huge fireplace. Sam glanced up when they entered and immediately stood, removing his reading glasses.

"So I'm assuming Cloe is the owner of the car I found parked out front when I got home from town this afternoon."

"Yes, sir," Rome said. "We went to College Station."

"College Station? What for?"

"I'll tell you as soon as Casey gets here."

It looked like Sam wanted to say something else, but instead he held out his hand. "Won't you sit down, Cloe? Can I get you something to drink?"

"No, thank you." She would have taken a chair, but Rome directed her to the couch Sam had been sitting on and sat down next to her. He stretched his arm along the back of the couch and his fingers gently caressed her shoulder. She knew he was only trying to ease her nerves, but her body didn't seem to know that. His touch made her feel hotter than the crackling fire.

There was an awkward silence. Cloe started to compliment the bronze sculpture of a cowboy when bootheels clicked along the hallway and Casey peeked his head in. He looked like he'd just woken up from a nap. His hair was messed and his eyes sleepy. Something that didn't go unnoticed by Sam.

"Have you been napping when you were supposed to be checking on the cattle out in the west pasture?"

"I checked on the cattle this morning in the freezing-assed rain." He grinned at Cloe. "Pardon my language." He looked back at his father. "Once I got back, I figured I had earned a hot shower and a nap." He moved into the room and held his hands out to the fire. "So what's this meeting about, big bro? And why is the lovely Miss Cloe Holiday being forced to join us?"

Much to Cloe's horror, Rome didn't mince words. "After this morning, it's Cloe Remington."

Casey whirled around and Sam almost dropped the book he still held. Cloe felt her cheeks heat. She sent an annoyed look at Rome, but he only shrugged while his brother and father gaped. Feeling like it was up to her to smooth things over, she forced a smile.

"I know this comes as a shock. We just thought you and my father would try to stop us if we told you."

Sam looked at Rome. "You should have talked to me first."

"Why?" Casey said. "Choosing Rome's wife isn't any of your—"

Rome cut in. "I got this, Case." He calmly looked at his father, but Cloe could feel the tension in his body. "You've been pushing me to get married. I got married. Like Casey was about to point out, you don't get to choose who."

"What happened to the son who told me he never wanted to get married again?"

Rome glanced at her and smiled. "I got to know Cloe." He pulled her closer and pressed a kiss on the side of her head. Her entire body flushed with heat and she knew her reaction was obvious when Sam spoke.

"Is she pregnant?"

She wasn't at all surprised by the question. She was sure her family would think the same thing. Especially if Mimi mentioned them spending the night in the hayloft. But before she could answer Sam, Casey spoke.

"Way to make everyone feel uncomfortable, Sam. And that's not any of our business either. If you're going to become a grandpa and I'm going to become an uncle, I'm sure Rome and Cloe will tell us when they're ready. Until then . . ." He walked over and took Cloe's hands, pulling her up from the couch and into his arms for a tight hug. "Welcome to the family, sis." He drew back and looked at Sam. "I think this calls for some of that expensive whiskey you keep hidden. Don't you . . . Daddy?"

Sam didn't look happy, but he didn't ask any more questions either. Which was a relief. Cloe had not wanted to straight-face lie to Rome's father. It was bad enough she would have to do it to her family. After Casey made a toast to the happy couple, Rome made their excuses and they headed over to the Holiday Ranch.

"Does your daddy own a shotgun?" Rome asked when they were standing on her front porch.

She grinned. "Now who's nervous?"

Since the weather was so nasty, she wasn't surprised to find Daddy and Mimi sitting in the living room watching *Wheel of Fortune*. She could hear her mother puttering around in the kitchen. No doubt making some kind of soup and home-made bread for dinner. Her mama always made soup and homemade bread on cold days.

"Well, it's about time you got home, Clover Fields," Mimi said when she saw her. "We've all been worried sick about you driving on these roads."

"Speak for yourself, Mama," Daddy said. "I wasn't worried. I taught all my girls to drive on ice. It was you two nervous nellies who wouldn't stop looking out the windows. And quit hovering in the door, Cloe. You're letting all the warm air out."

Cloe stepped in, and Rome followed closely behind her.

He pulled off his hat and smiled. "Hey, y'all."

Mimi's eyes narrowed. "Rome Remington. Well, this is a surprise."

"And not a good one," Daddy grumbled as he got to his feet.

"Hush, Hank." Mama came out of the kitchen, drying her hands on a dish towel. "Thank good-ness you're back, Cloe. I was worried sick." She smiled at Rome. "So nice to see you, Rome. Did you run into Cloe in town on her way back from College Station?"

Before Rome had to answer, Cloe spoke. "Actu-ally, he went with me to College Station." She cleared her throat, wondering how she should broach the subject. "Maybe we should sit down."

"I'm not sittin' down," Daddy said as his eyes

narrowed on Rome. "Just spit it out, Clover Fields."

So much for trying to ease into things. She sighed. "Rome and I got married."

Mama gasped. Daddy growled. And Mimi, for once, didn't say a word. But there was a gloating gleam in her eyes.

"What the hell were you thinking?" Daddy said before he turned to Mimi. "This is all your fault, Mama. If you hadn't put your harebrained scheme in her head, she wouldn't now be wed to a Remington." He looked at Rome. "And if you think I'm going to let my mama give you this ranch, you got another think coming."

"Of course, I'm going to give him this ranch," Mimi piped up. "A deal is a deal. I'm not a woman to go back on my word. But before I hand it over, I'll need proof."

"We have it." Cloe reached in her purse and pulled out the marriage license, but Mimi shook her head.

"I'm not talking about that kind of proof. I mean I'm not signing anything until I'm sure this is a love match."

CHAPTER TWELVE

IT WAS LATE by the time Rome and Cloe left the Holiday Ranch. Cloe's mama had insisted they stay for supper. Rome felt awkward sitting at the table while Hank glared at him, but the food made up for it. If Cloe cooked anything like Darla Holiday, Rome was looking forward to the next few months.

Or possibly longer.

Mimi wasn't planning on just signing the ranch over, even after Rome had told her she'd have the money to pay off the loan by Monday. He grinned. The old gal had what his Grandfather Remington had called moxie. Which was where Cloe had gotten it. Marrying him was the last thing she'd wanted to do, but she'd done it. She'd done it for her family.

Damn, he admired her for that.

Although it looked like deceiving her family had completely drained her. She sat in the passenger's seat with her head resting on the headrest as she stared at the icy rain hitting the windshield. He figured she wasn't just drained from having to tell their families about their marriage, but also about discovering Brandon had a girlfriend.

He wanted to reach across the console and take her hand, but he didn't want to blur the lines of their business deal. Still, he couldn't help feeling concerned.

"I guess you're upset over Brandon."

"Actually, I haven't given him much thought." She hesitated. "I've been too upset about lying to my family."

"We didn't lie. Your family knows exactly why we got married. I think my brother does too. Mimi made him the same offer as she made me. My daddy will figure it out as soon as Mimi signs over the ranch . . . if she signs over the ranch."

"She'll sign it over. She just wants to make sure we aren't fooling her." She sighed. "I hate deceiving her. She's convinced she's going to get grandchildren out of this."

Like Cloe, he hated to deceive the older woman, but he couldn't see any way around it. "She's going to get grandchildren. I'm sure your sisters will have kids. And you too. It's not like marrying me will stop you from finding the right man once we're divorced."

"The right man." She laughed, but there was no joy in it.

"You don't sound very positive, Lucky. Just because you wasted a lot of years on the wrong guy, doesn't mean you should give up."

She turned her head to look at him. "And what about you? You gave up."

"I'm different."

"How so?"

Maybe it was the defeated look in her eyes. Or maybe it was the need to finally put his feelings into words. But whatever the reason, he told her something he'd never told another soul.

"The difference is that you still believe in love. I don't. Love didn't keep Emily from leaving. And it sure as hell didn't keep my mama from walking out on her husband and two sons. Therefore, I'm not willing to waste my time searching for something as fickle and untrustworthy as love."

When she didn't say anything, he glanced over to find her looking at him with eyes that glimmered like the ice crystals sticking to the windshield.

"I'm sorry," she said.

A fist tightened around his heart and again he had the strong desire to reach out and touch her. Instead, he looked back at the highway. "Me too."

They didn't talk after that. When he pulled into the garage, he glanced over to find her fast asleep. Her hair was even more curly from the humidity and looked like a wild lion's mane. Her glasses had slid down her nose and precariously hung from the tip. And her mouth was slightly open, a soft snore huffing out. He got out and walked around to her side. He thought opening the door and unbuckling her seat belt would wake her, but she slept right through it. If she'd been like him, she'd gotten very little sleep the night before.

He slid her glasses up on her nose before he gently lifted her out of the seat. She barely weighed more than a couple fifty-pound bags of horse feed. He bumped the truck door closed with his shoulder before he carried her toward the laundry room door. As he was stepping over the threshold, a memory filtered into his mind. A memory of another wedding night where he carried his bride over the threshold. But Emily had been awake and they'd been kissing as he'd carried her up the stairs to their bed.

Tonight, there would be no kissing tonight.

No lovemaking.

No their bed.

He planned to sleep on a blow-up mattress he'd bought on Amazon in the room connected to the master suite. His father had given him the suite after he'd married Emily. When Rome was born, Sam had enlarged the master bathroom and added a door that led to Rome's nursery. He had hoped Rome and Emily would use it as a nursery too. Instead, Rome had turned it into an office.

Now it would be his room for the next few months.

Suddenly, his joy at having a woman in the house dimmed.

"She sleeping?"

Casey stood at the top of the stairs.

Rome nodded as he climbed the last step. "It's been a tough day."

"I bet." Casey hurried ahead of him down the hallway and opened Rome's bedroom door.

Rome carried Cloe in and carefully laid her on the large king-sized bed. He slipped off her snow boots, and then covered her with the fuzzy throw blanket he kept on the end. She didn't rouse at all. Not even when he removed her glasses and set them on the nightstand.

"I guess your honeymoon will have to wait."

He turned to see Casey standing in the doorway. He wasn't smiling. His expression was serious.

"Or will there be a honeymoon?"

Rome tucked the blanket more securely around Cloe before he walked out of the room and closed the door behind him. Since his father's room was just down the hall and he didn't want Sam overhearing their conversation, he motioned for Casey to follow him to his office. Once there, he sat down in the chair behind the desk and ran his hands over his face.

"I wanted the land and Mimi wouldn't sell it otherwise."

"I figured as much. So the wily old woman's plan worked."

Rome glanced up to see Casey grinning like a Cheshire cat. He couldn't help laughing. "I guess it did. Did you know she owns the ranch?"

"Mimi?"

Rome nodded. "Lock, stock, and barrel."

Casey shook his head. "If I'd known she had the power to sign over the ranch, I might have married me a Holiday and given her those grandkids she's wanting."

"There will be no grandkids. Cloe and I aren't going to stay married."

"Hmm?"

"What does that mean?"

Casey shrugged. "Just that Cloe's a beautiful woman and you're a man who hasn't had sex in a very lo-o-ong time. Babies happen. Mimi is smart enough to know that."

"Well, they're not happening with us. I'm sleeping right here."

Casey glanced at the connecting door. "I give you a couple weeks and you'll be trying to sneak your way through that door."

"Not happening."

"Like Granny Remington used to say, the best-laid plans . . ."

Rome woke up the following morning with a major kink in his neck. He'd slept even worse than he had the night before. Due to the fact that the air mattress seemed to be losing air and now looked like a marshmallow left too long over a hot coal. It was a struggle to get up from it. He spent a few minutes trying to stretch the kink out. When that didn't work, he headed to the bathroom to take a shower.

Since the master bathroom was situated between the two bedrooms, he figured it wouldn't be a problem sharing it with Cloe. He loved his big shower with the double showerheads and didn't want to give it up. Being that he got up at the crack of dawn, he figured he could get his morning shower in before she even woke up.

But when he opened the bathroom door, he realized Cloe was an early riser too. She stood in front of the sink, brushing her teeth . . . as naked as the day she was born.

All Rome could do was stare at all the glorious flesh exposed for his viewing pleasure. He not only had a side view, but also a half frontal in the reflection of the large mirror over the double sinks. Her breasts hung like two ripe melons from the vine, their large nipples the prettiest pink he'd ever seen in his life. Her waist he could easily span with two hands. Unfortunately, the sink and cabinet blocked the front of her from the waist down. But behind, her hips flared out in lush curves that made his hands itch, and her legs were toned and long enough to make a man dream about being snuggled between them.

A startled gasp pulled him from the hot fantasy and he lifted his gaze to see Cloe's wide eyes reflected in the mirror. Her toothbrush dropped from her hand and fell in the sink as she hunched and tried to cover her breasts with her hands. With all that abundant flesh, it was an impossible task. He didn't realize he was still standing there staring until she yelled.

"Get out!"

"Excuse me," he quickly muttered before he stepped back and pulled the door closed. He stood there for a long moment, the image of Cloe naked burned onto his retinas. All he could think was . . .

Shit. I'm in big trouble.

He ended up taking a shower in the main level guest bathroom. On his way back up the stairs to get his clothes, he ran into Cloe coming down. It was an awkward moment. Especially when he only wore a towel and her sweater and jeans couldn't hide the curves he now knew were there. He kept his gaze above her neck and cleared his throat.

"Good mornin'." He decided it would be best to address the elephant on the stairs. "I'm sorry about earlier. I guess we need to put together a bathroom schedule."

She glanced down at his naked chest and then quickly back up. Her cheeks blushed a pretty pink. "I should have locked the door. I didn't realize it went to another room. I thought it was a towel closet."

"I planned to give you the tour when we got back, but you were sleeping so soundly, I didn't want to wake you."

"You should have. You shouldn't have . . . carried me to bed."

He shrugged and would have said it was no problem if pain hadn't shot through his neck, causing him to cringe.

"You're hurt," she said.

He rubbed his neck. "I just slept wrong."

"Don't lie, Rome. You pulled something when you carried me up these stairs." She took his arm, her gentle touch burning him like a hot brand. "Turn around. Let me see if I can rub it out."

The last thing he needed was Cloe rubbing on him. "No, thank you. I'm good."

"No, you're not. You're holding your head at an awkward angle. Now, turn around."

He did what she asked and she moved to a higher stair and started massaging his shoulders. He thought she would massage like she touched—gently with no pressure at all. But there was nothing gentle about the way Cloe dug the pads of her fingers into his muscles. It hurt like hell, for a second, then it felt like he'd died and gone to heaven.

His head fell limply forward as he released a groan of sheer pleasure.

"Feel good?"

"Mmm," was all he could get out as she kneaded his neck and then down to his shoulder blades.

"There it is. Just let me work this knot out."

At that moment, he would let her do anything she wanted as long as she kept touching him. She had magic fingers. They seemed to know exactly where to press . . . and how hard to squeeze.

That thought was all it took for his mind to wander down a porn path. Suddenly, images of her massaging a lot more than his shoulders and neck popped into his head. Images of her squeezing his pectoral muscles, and then pinching his nipples hard. Images of her roughly kneading his ass cheeks and tightly gripping his—

"Good mornin'!"

At Casey's bright greeting, Rome snapped out of his fantasy and almost took a header down the stairs. He caught himself and turned to find his brother standing there grinning like a cat who had just swallowed the canary.

"Good morning," Cloe said. "I was just giving your brother a massage. He has a kink in his neck."

"Now isn't that a shame." Casey glanced down and arched one eyebrow. "But it looks like that massage perked him right up."

Rome followed his brother's gaze and realized what Casey was referring to. He'd pitched a towel tent. And unfortunately, Cloe had followed his brother's gaze too.

"Oh!" She quickly looked away. "E–E–Excuse me. I forgot something." She turned and hurried back to her room, leaving Rome to glare at his brother.

Casey only smiled. "Make that one week."

CHAPTER THIRTEEN

THE HOLIDAY SECRET Sisterhood had started after Belle had read the book *Divine Secrets of the Ya-Ya Sisterhood* when she was in middle school and decided the Holiday sisters needed to have their own secret society. When they were teens, they held the meetings in the hayloft and talked about boys, school, and their stubborn daddy. After they all left home, they had the meetings on Zoom and talked about everything from jobs to boys . . . to their stubborn daddy.

But this morning, the topic was Cloe getting married.

"I told everyone Cloe wasn't okay after Brandon broke up with her." Liberty's voice boomed through Cloe's laptop speaker. "But did anyone listen to me. No-o-o. And now look what's happened. She's gone along with Mimi's ridiculous scheme and married a Remington!"

Belle, who sat right next to Liberty, patted her arm. "Calm down, Libby. Yelling is not going to help the situation." She looked into the camera. "But what were you thinking, Cloe?"

Before Cloe could answer, Sweetie spoke. "She was thinking about saving the ranch."

"By marrying a man she doesn't even like?" Liberty said.

"I like Rome." It was true. She did like Rome. The more she got to know him, the more she liked him. She and Rome were a lot alike. They were even tempered, logical, and practical. Which was how they had ended up where they were. Marrying was the logical, practical thing to do. Even if her sisters didn't agree.

"You don't get married just because you like someone," Noelle said. "What about love?"

The question made her think about Rome's declaration. *I've lost my faith in love.* His reasons for losing his faith had touched her heart, but they had also made sense.

Love *was* fickle.

"I'm not so sure I trust love anymore," she said. "It certainly hasn't worked for me."

"Because Brandon was a jackass!" Hallie bellowed. She was in the basement of the apartment building she lived in. No doubt working on a new recipe for the perfect beer. "Rome, on the other hand, is hot, rich, and a badass rancher. People think the Remington Ranch is so successful because of Sam. But after talking to Rome at the reception, I think he's the one behind the ranch's success. Did you know he has a master's degree in business?"

Cloe didn't know that. It made her realize how much she didn't know about the man she was married to.

"I, for one, don't think Cloe made a bad choice at all," Hallie continued. "She got a hot cowboy, Daddy's debt paid off, and we get to keep the house. How is that a bad thing?"

"Because our sister is stuck in a loveless marriage for the rest of her life with a land-hungry Remington," Noelle said.

Cloe hadn't planned on telling her sisters the truth, but she couldn't let them continue to worry about her. Her mama and daddy worrying was more than enough. Mimi wasn't worried at all. She was convinced Cloe had made the right choice and with time love would come. But there would be no time. Something she needed to tell her sisters.

"I'm not staying married to Rome."

Five pairs of wide eyes stared back at her from her laptop screen. Liberty was the first to snap out of it and laugh. "Why, you devious little con artist. I didn't think you had it in you."

"You planned this entire thing?" Sweetie asked.

"Planned what?" Noelle leaned closer to the camera, a whisk in her hand. "I don't get it."

Hallie threw her hands in the air. "Good Lord, Elle, pull your head out of your social media fantasy world. Cloe married Rome to get Mimi to sell the ranch. As soon as he pays off Daddy's debt and gets the land, Cloe will get a divorce."

Noelle blinked. "But that's really mean. Mimi is counting on keeping our land in the family. She's going to be heartbroken."

"Well, she would have been even more heart

broken if she had lost her house and the land," Sweetie said. "Which is exactly what would have happened if Cloe hadn't stepped in." She paused, a worried frown on her face. "But I still don't know if this was a good idea, Clo. A lot can go wrong. Is Rome in on this?"

"It was his idea."

"Told you he was smart," Hallie said. "And I bet it pissed his daddy off to no end that his son married a Holiday. Our daddy is fit to be tied."

"If Sam is upset, he hasn't shown it," Cloe said. "Of course, I get the feeling the Remingtons don't share their emotions easily."

Noelle snorted. "Not Casey. He shows his emotions to every girl in town."

"Ple-e-ease," Hallie said. "Can you just shut up about Casey Remington already? We get it. You hate him. This isn't about your weird obsession with Casey. It's about Cloe taking one for the team." She bumped the camera with her fist. "Way to go, Clo."

"Amen," Liberty said. "I couldn't have come up with a better plan myself. If I was you, I'd get Mimi to sign over the ranch as soon as possible. You don't want her finding out you and Rome tricked her until it's too late for her to do anything about it."

Cloe cringed at just the thought of her grandmother finding out. "I don't want her ever finding out. Or Mama and Daddy either. I think they both know why I did what I did, but they still think wedding vows are sacred and should be kept. As does almost every person in town. Which is why y'all need to promise to never tell a soul I planned to divorce Rome all along."

"Of course we won't," Belle said. "But we still should take an oath." She placed one hand over her heart and lifted her other. "As a sister of the Holiday Secret Sisterhood, I pledge to never tell anyone about Cloe and Rome's plan or I will be banned from the sisterhood forever."

The rest of her sisters lifted their hands and repeated after her.

Hallie leaned closer to the camera. "So now for the juicy details. Is sex part of this fake marriage?"

Since Rome caught her naked in the bathroom and the incident on the stairs, Cloe had tried her best to keep all sexual thoughts about Rome out of her head. She had failed miserably. At the most inopportune times images popped into her brain. An image of his hungry eyes when she'd caught him looking at her in the bathroom. Another of his lean, muscled body in nothing but a white towel . . . with an obvious tent. Not only did the images leave her feeling flushed and needy, but they also left her with one question.

Did Rome desire her?

"Well, I don't see why sex is off the table." Liberty cut into Cloe's thoughts. "If you have to live with him, you might as well enjoy it."

"Stop, Libby," Belle chastised. "I'm sure Cloe is still too upset over Brandon to be interested in Rome."

Cloe had been upset. But since running into Brandon and Sabrina at the coffee shop, she'd become more angry than upset. And anger was easier to deal with than hurt.

"Actually," she said. "I'm over Brandon. Hallie was right. He is a selfish, arrogant asshole. And I'm better off without him."

"Woot!" Hallie punched the air. "See, if everyone would just listen to me, they'd be much better off. Now let's go back to you doing the nasty with—"

Before she could finish, Casey walked into the kitchen. "Hey, sis! I thought you might want to go riding so I saddled you up a horse and Lady Grantham is waiting out—" He cut off when he saw the screen of her laptop. "Whoa! Now there is a fine selection of beautiful women if ever I saw one." He pulled off his hat as he leaned over Cloe's shoulder. "Good afternoon, ladies."

"Hey, Casey!" her sisters chorused . . . everyone but Noelle, who just glared.

If he noticed, Casey didn't let on. "I guess you heard I'm your new outlaw."

Liberty laughed. "Outlaw?"

"I'm not your in-law, but I figure I'm close enough to still be considered family."

"You're not part of my family," Noelle grumbled before she disappeared from the screen. The rest of her sisters chatted with Casey for a few minutes before they said their goodbyes.

Cloe and Casey spent the rest of the morning riding around the ranch. She didn't know what she enjoyed more—being back in the saddle or listening to Casey's stories about he and Rome growing up on the ranch. The brothers seemed to be as close as she was to her sisters. It sounded like they'd had just as much fun together. What was lacking from the stories was any mention of Sam. Cloe had to wonder if Casey and Rome had pretty much been on their own. While she had plenty of stories about the time she spent with her sisters, she also had plenty of stories about the things she'd done with her entire family. But if Mimi and her mama hadn't been there to soften her daddy's sternness, she knew her life would have been much different.

When they got back to the house, she offered to make Casey lunch. Unfortunately, there wasn't much to work with in the refrigerator and pantry.

"Sorry," Casey said. "Rome usually goes to the grocery store." He sent her an impish look. "But he's been a little busy this week."

"I don't mind going." She found a couple slices of cheese in the back of the deli drawer and took them out. "I have to go into town today anyway. I want to stop by the elementary school and see if there's any openings for a speech therapist."

Casey pulled out a half loaf of bread from the breadbox. "So you're planning on staying here in Wilder after you and Rome split up?"

She stopped unwrapping the cheese slices and turned to him. "Rome told you?"

"He didn't have to. Your grandmother made me the same offer and I knew my brother had no plans to remarry again. Not after Emily broke his heart."

It wasn't any of her business, but she still couldn't help asking. "What happened with Emily?"

He pulled a knife out of a drawer and started buttering slices of bread. "I think she thought being a wealthy rancher's wife was going to be a lot more glamorous than it is. She wasn't used to the isolation of a ranch. Rome tried to take her into Austin as much as possible, but it wasn't enough. She missed her big city life and finally just left."

Cloe started assembling the sandwiches while Casey pulled out a pan. "Did Rome try going after her?"

Casey shook his head. "That's not really my daddy's and Rome's style. If you hurt them, you're pretty much dead to them. Rome won't even talk to our mama."

Cloe was more than surprised. She had thought their mother was completely out of the picture. Probably because Rome never mentioned her. "Your mother has tried to contact y'all?"

"She started calling a few years ago. I talk to her, but Rome refuses to. Mama thinks it's because he has a cold heart like Daddy. But I think it's just the opposite. I think the more fragile your heart, the more you guard it. Rome has put up plenty of guards around his heart all because he doesn't want to get hurt again." For once, Casey's face was serious when he looked at her. "And I don't want that either."

She knew the last statement was directed at her. Casey was trying to protect his brother.

"I won't hurt him, Casey. This marriage isn't real and we both know it."

After they finished eating lunch, Casey went

back to work while Cloe took inventory of the refrigerator, freezer, and pantry and made a shopping list before she headed into town. She was browsing the meat section at the general store when Mrs. Stokes came around the corner of the aisle, pushing a squeaky cart.

Cloe had always been terrified of the woman so she quickly pretended to be engrossed with selecting a chuck roast, in the hopes Mrs. Stokes wouldn't see her and roll her cart right on by.

She wasn't that lucky.

"Why, if it isn't the new Mrs. Remington."

It wasn't shocking she already knew about Cloe and Rome getting married. Mrs. Stokes was a friend of Mimi's. And Mimi had no doubt broadcasted the news as soon as she woke up this morning. She was thrilled her plan had worked.

Cloe turned and pinned on a smile. "Hello, Ms. Stokes. How are you doing? Just getting a little shopping done?"

"I'm cooking for my boyfriend, Jeffrey, tonight." Mrs. Stokes glanced down at her basket that held a pile of produce in plastic bags. "He's one of those folks who doesn't eat meat." She shook her head. "That would be a deal breaker if he wasn't so damn good at foot massages. The other night, he did something to the arch of my foot that almost had me asking him to marry me. And I have no desire to get married again." She winked at Cloe. "Of course, Rome didn't either and it only took one night in the hayloft with you to change his mind."

Cloe's eyes widened. "Mimi told you about the hayloft?"

"She didn't have to. I was the one who pointed Rome in the right direction when he was lookin' for you." She chortled and then went into a deep, phlegmy cough that lasted so long Cloe was able to pick out a large chuck roast before it was finished.

"Nothing happened in the hayloft, Ms. Stokes," she said as she put the roast in her cart.

"Oh, something happened." Mrs. Stokes gaze grew intent. "Something had to happen to make two people who had never paid much attention to each other decide to get married. Since you and Rome have always put your families first, I think I can figure out what that something was." A smile spread over her face. "But just so you know, even the best laid plans don't always turn out the way you think they will. Sometimes they turn out worse . . . and sometimes they turn out better."

Mrs. Stokes winked before she headed down the aisle with her squeaky cart.

CHAPTER FOURTEEN

ROME WAS BONE tired by the time he got home late that night. He'd spent the day dealing with the aftermath of the ice storm. The cattle had all survived, but in the late morning one of the ranch hands had discovered an oak tree had fallen and taken down a fence in the east pasture. Not only did they have to round up the cattle that had gotten out, but they had to clear the huge tree that had come up by its roots, fill in the hole so no cows would fall in it, and then fix the fence.

"Damn that was a tough day," Casey said as they stood in the mudroom taking off their coats and muddy boots.

"You weren't even there for half of it," Sam grumbled.

"I told you I was showing Cloe around the ranch."

Rome felt the same annoyance he'd felt earlier when Casey had told him what he'd been doing. That annoyance grew when he continued.

"And I'll tell you what. She's a damned fine horsewoman." Casey tugged off his boot. "She had no trouble keeping up with me. She even helped me herd a calf back to its mama. When we got back to the ranch, she insisted on taking care of Lady Grantham. She unsaddled her and rubbed her down. Lady's smitten with her already." He grinned at Rome. "Of course, so am I."

Rome didn't laugh. "Shut up, Casey. I'm too tired to deal with your bullshit tonight."

"Ooo, did I hit a sensitive spot, bro? If you weren't going to take the time to show your new bride around, I figured someone should."

"That's enough, Casey," Sam said. "Let's get something to eat and get to bed. We have a long day of branding tomorrow."

There wouldn't be much to eat. Rome was the only one who went to the grocery store and he'd been a little busy. So he was surprised when he stepped into the kitchen and smelled something that made his stomach grumble with hunger. "What is that? It smells like . . ."

"Pie!" Casey strode over to the counter where what looked like a blackberry pie sat. "It's official." He leaned down and took a deep whiff of the pie. "I'm in love with your wife."

Rome's stomach growled as he moved closer to the counter and saw the oozing blackberries and flaky crust. There was a note sitting next to the pie.

Dinner is in the refrigerator. It just needs to be heated.

Casey read it at the same time as he did and let out a hoot of joy as he raced to the refrigerator. Dinner turned out to be pot roast and tiny little carrots in dark, rich gravy. Mashed potatoes and green beans were in separate containers.

Once they had filled their plates and heated them in the microwave, all three men hunkered down at the island and shoveled the delicious meal into their mouths. Even Sam looked like he was in heaven. Especially when the pie was divvied out.

"She can cook," Sam said. "I'll give her that much."

"Wait a second." Casey stared at their father. "Did Sam Remington just give a Holiday a compliment?"

Sam didn't comment. He was too busy eating pie.

Once they were finished eating, exhaustion set in. Since Casey hadn't exactly put in a full day, Rome left him to do the dishes while he and Sam headed up to bed. When they reached the top of the stairs, Sam looked at him.

"I wasn't much on you marrying a Holiday, but if you get that land, it might not be a bad deal."

Even though it was the truth, there was something about the way his father said it that didn't set well with Rome.

"It's not just about the land."

Sam's eyebrows rose. "Don't tell me it's love."

It wasn't, but for some reason, he didn't want his father to know that. "It's not just about the land," he repeated before he turned and headed down the hallway.

He was dead tired, but when he passed his room and saw the light coming from beneath the door, he stopped and tapped softly. Cloe answered almost immediately. Her hair was braided in one long rope that hung over her shoulder. She was dressed in flannel pajamas that were covered in four-leaf clovers the same color as her eyes. Emily had always greeted him with anger when he'd worked late and missed dinner. Cloe's eyes held nothing but relief.

"You're home." Her choice of words caused his chest to feel tight and he had to wonder if he should've eaten that second piece of pie. Her gaze raked over him from head to toe and he knew he must look like hell. "I guess it was a tough day. How's your neck? I got you some ointment to rub on it at the general store. Mr. Crawley swears it makes his sore muscles feel better. I left it on the counter in the bathroom. You should take a hot shower and rub some on."

He was so stunned by her kindness it took him a moment to find words. "Thank you. For the ointment and for supper. It was . . . good." *Good.* That's all he could come up with? Damn, he *was* tired.

Cloe didn't seem offended. "I'm glad you liked it." They stood there for an awkward moment before she cleared her throat. "Well, I guess I'll see you tomorrow."

"Yeah. See you tomorrow." He waved weirdly before he turned and headed to his room.

He almost fell asleep against the shower wall while standing under the hot spray. After toweling off, he applied the ointment. It heated beneath his fingers and, with just a few kneading strokes, his neck started to feel better. Of course, if he didn't want to wake up with it worse in the morning, he needed to add more air to the mattress.

Once in his room, he pulled on a pair of boxer briefs before he attached the small air compressor the mattress had come with to the opening on the side and turned it on. Figuring he'd be able to tell how much air it needed better if he was lying on it, he climbed onto the mattress and waited for it to reach the right firmness.

The next thing he knew, he woke to a loud ripping sound and a rush of escaping air as the mattress sank around him. While he was lying there encased in deflated plastic, the connecting door opened and Cloe rushed in.

"Rome? Are you okay? What was that sound?"

"I'm fine. But I don't think my mattress is." He reached over the lump of plastic and turned off the compressor just as the overhead light came on. He squinted until his eyes focused.

Cloe stood over him with her hand over her mouth and her eyes twinkling with suppressed laughter. Rome figured he looked damn silly lying in a puddle of deflated plastic. A giggle escaped through her fingers. More giggles followed until she was holding her sides. He couldn't help smiling. She looked damn cute in those clover pajamas with her braid and her eyes dancing as she gasped for breath.

"It's just—that—you look—like a—swaddled—baby."

"A swaddled baby? I feel more like a hot dog in a bun."

She continued to laugh. "Peas—in—a—pod."

He fought his way out of the plastic and sat up. "How can I be peas when I'm only one person. Now if you were to get in here with me, then we'd be peas in a pod." She stopped laughing and he realized what he'd just said. "Not that I'm inviting you into my bed."

Her smile returned. "I wouldn't call that a bed."

He laughed. "Good point. I guess I'll be sleeping on the couch tonight."

"You can't sleep on the couch or you really will have a crick in your neck. And what about your father? He'll think we had a fight." Rome started to tell her his father knew why they had gotten married, but before he could, she continued. "You can sleep with me. Your bed is huge and it's not like we haven't slept together before." Without waiting for a reply, she turned and headed back through the bathroom.

He got up with every intention of following her and telling her he wasn't going to share a bed with her. But when he got into the room and found her snuggled under the covers just like she'd been snuggled in the blanket in the hayloft, with her braid spilling over the pillow and her green eyes innocent and direct, all the words he'd been going to say died a quick death.

He realized he wanted to climb into bed with her much more than he wanted to go downstairs and sleep on the couch.

It wasn't sexual—he was too damn tired to think about sex. It was a deeper need. A need he'd pushed way down deep after Emily left. A need to sleep next to someone and listen to their breathing and know that he wasn't alone.

Without a word, he walked back into his office and switched off the light before he returned and climbed into bed. She waited until he was tucked under the covers before she turned off the lamp. Once the room was pitch black, awkwardness set in. Maybe he should put a pillow between them. Just to keep them on their sides of the bed. She must have been thinking the same thing because a moment later he felt a pillow brush his arm.

"I could sleep with Casey," he said.

"No. It's fine."

"Good, because he snores worse than you do."

"I snore?"

"Only softly."

Her voice held a smile. "How very unchivalrous of you."

"Unchivalrous? Is that even a word?"

"Are you questioning a speech therapist?"

"Never."

She giggled. "Well, you're right. It's not a word."

He chuckled. He liked this mischievous side of Cloe. "Do you miss working with kids?"

"I do. I love everything about my job. I know what it's like to have difficulty communicating. Seeing the look on a child's face when they overcome their speech impediments is the most amazing feeling in the world. I applied today at Wilder Elementary. They don't have an opening now, but they will in the fall."

He turned on his side, but regretted it when he realized she was lying on her side facing him.

Even with the pillow between them, it was intimate. But there was no way to roll back over without looking like a fool. So he ignored the scent of warm woman and tried to keep his mind on their conversation. "You're planning on staying here?"

"I think it's the right thing to do. Even if I stayed in College Station, I'd be transferring schools in the fall. And if I stay here after the divorce, Mimi won't be so upset and disappointed with me."

"Mimi won't be disappointed with you. I think I've proven I'm the one no woman can live with."

"That's not true, Rome. A marriage takes two people to make it work. And I don't know why your mama left, but I'm sure it wasn't because of something an innocent child did."

He knew she was right, but deep down he couldn't help believing there was something in him that was unlovable. Something that pushed women away. But he wasn't about to tell Cloe that.

Yet, somehow, she knew.

She reached over the pillow and placed a hand on his arm. The gentle warmth of her fingers was more than just soothing. They made the knot of hurt he had carried around for so long feel less tight.

"It's not your fault, Rome. You need to let that go."

He didn't remember falling asleep. When he woke it was to soft snoring, the scent of springtime, and a feeling of contentment. He opened his eyes to sunlight shining in through the cracks in the curtains, fanning his ceiling in rays of gold. He started to stretch like he did every morning when he realized his left arm was imprisoned. He looked down to see Cloe draped over his chest, her hair tickling his chin.

He wanted to blame her for encroaching on his side, but he was on her side, the pillow barrier at the foot of the bed. Not wanting her to wake up and find him there, he tried to carefully ease her off his chest so he could scoot over to his side before she woke up. But he only shifted her a few inches when she stopped snoring and hummed contentedly before snuggling closer to his chest, her lips brushing his nipple.

There had been no sexual thoughts last night. This morning, his brain and body made up for it. A mammoth wave of desire rolled thorough him, causing so much blood to rush to his cock he felt lightheaded. To make matters worse, she chose that moment to wake up.

She must have realized the situation they were in because she sucked in her breath and froze. She remained that way for a long moment before her hand moved. He thought she was preparing to slip away from him. Instead, her fingers caressed the hair on his chest.

He inhaled sharply and her head quickly lifted. He found himself looking into meadow-green eyes. Meadow-green eyes that held the same heat that coiled around him.

With a groan, he fisted his fingers in her loose braid and pulled her to his waiting lips. If there had been any kind of hesitation on her part, he might have been able to stop. But there wasn't. As soon as their lips met, they melted into a frenzied dance of hot slides and tangled tongues. She shifted so she was fully on top of him, her hips undulating against his hard length. Any thought of keeping their relationship purely platonic evaporated. He wanted in those shamrock pajamas and he wanted in them now.

Still, his brain made one last weak effort.

"We should probably stop," he whispered as he sucked on her plump bottom lip.

"Yes. We need to stop." She kissed him again, her tongue playful and hot. He slipped his hand under her top, filling his palm with lush, warm breast. He stroked his thumb over a nipple so hard that it made him groan deep in his chest.

She pulled back from the kiss, her breath as harsh and uneven as his as her hips pumped restlessly. "We should really keep a firm boundary."

"Firm." He slipped his hands into her pajama bottoms, cupping her butt cheeks as he rubbed his straining erection against her.

A little choked sob came out of her mouth and she pressed closer. "Because—this—isn't real."

"Not real," he echoed. But damn it felt real. More real than anything he had felt in a long time. He felt like he could come from just the friction they were creating. He wanted more. He needed more.

"Sit up," he ordered.

She complied, straddling him with her hair wild around her shoulders. He feverishly undid the buttons of her pajama top, pushing back the edges to reveal her abundant breasts hanging like sweet fruit in the morning light.

He groaned as he filled his palms with each one and lifted them. Unable to resist the overflowing bounty, he raised his head and rained open-mouth kisses over the soft flesh before pulling one sweet crest into his mouth. She arched her back, her fingers scraping along his scalp before they fisted tightly in his hair.

"Rome."

His name coming from her lips in that breath-less tone made him twice as hard. He laved his tongue over her nipple wanting to hear her say it again and again. She didn't, but her satisfied sighs and moans were just as good. He could have feasted on her breasts forever if one of her hands hadn't found its way into his briefs. Just like with her massage, she wasn't gentle. She fisted him firmly as she stroked him from base to moist tip.

He looked down. The sight of her long fingers with their neatly trimmed nails curled around his hard cock was about the hottest thing he'd ever seen. His breath left his lungs as he watched her fist-pump him.

But he didn't want to lose it without her being right there with him.

He released her breasts and rolled her to her side. Slipping his hand into her pajama bottoms, his fingers easily finding her hot, wet folds. When he located the nub at the top of her clit, she sucked in her breath and her hand tightened on his cock. The closer she got to coming the tighter she held him. When she gasped out his name and climaxed, he covered her hand with his and pumped out his own.

The feeling of utopic satisfaction was quickly followed by the realization of what they'd done. Or more like what he'd done. He was the one who had removed the pillow. The one who hadn't been able to resist kissing her.

The one who had completely obliterated the boundary he'd set.

CHAPTER FIFTEEN

IT WAS EASY to read the look of regret in Rome's eyes.

Cloe instantly felt like a fool. She should have never invited him into her bed. But he'd looked so exhausted after he'd gotten home and she couldn't stand the thought of him having to sleep on the couch. It wasn't like they hadn't slept together before.

But that was when they were still strangers. Before she'd realized the type of man he was. A man who was willing to pretend to be her childhood sweetheart so she wouldn't lose face in front of her ex. A man who could laugh at himself when lying in a popped air mattress. A man who blamed himself for his mama and wife leaving him. A man who kissed her like no man had ever kissed her before.

As soon as his lips had touched hers, she'd been lost.

And maybe she'd been lost sooner than that.

Ever since grade school, she'd been aware of Rome. She'd known exactly how his hair curled at the collar of his shirts and the angle he wore his hat. She'd known his favorite brand of jeans, boots, and trucks, and how he ate his muffins.

If she were honest with herself, her preoccupation with Rome had been going on for a long time. Now that she'd gotten to know him that awareness had grown.

She now knew his scent was a mixture of fresh country air, saddle leather, and hardworking man. She knew he was hot natured and rarely needed a coat. He had strong hands that were also gentle. Could dance like nobody's business. And had skilled lips that could make her forget who she was and what this was—a fake marriage to a man who had told her himself that he didn't believe in love.

She knew that was where his regret came from. He was worried she would think this meant more than it did.

She needed to prove to him, and to herself, that it didn't.

She pulled her pajama top closed and forced a smile. "I guess I was wrong. I guess we can't sleep together."

He opened his mouth, but then closed it again. He sat up and ran a hand through his mussed hair. Her fingers tingled with the need to touch those thick glossy strands. "I'm sorry, Cloe. I take full responsibility for everything that happened. I was the one who trespassed on your side of the bed. The one who kissed you."

She sat up and buttoned her top. "And I kissed you back. So you aren't going to take all the blame. And it wasn't like we had sex. We just had . . ." She struggled to find a word and could only come up with one. "Release."

He quirked an eyebrow. "Release?" A smile spread over his face. "We did have that." He hesitated. "I just don't want you thinking that—"

"You've fallen madly in love with me?"

He sighed. "I was going to say I don't want you to think that this was part of my plan."

"I believe it was my idea to have you sleep in here. So I hope you don't think that getting you into bed was my plan."

"I would never think that about you, Cloe Holiday."

"And I don't think it about you."

He hesitated for a long moment before he spoke. "So we're good?"

"We're good."

His gaze traveled down to her breasts before it quickly lifted. "I guess we'd better stick to separate beds."

"I guess we better. Although, like I said before, I wouldn't call that puddle of plastic in the other room a bed."

He chuckled. "I'll order a new mattress today—a regular mattress. I think I'm through with air mattresses."

A knock sounded on the door and Casey's voice came through the wood.

"Hey, Cloe. You up?"

Rome's eyes widened and he quickly shook his head.

She held back her laughter. "I'm up. What did you need, Casey?"

"Have you seen Rome? He wasn't in his room and his air mattress looks like a deflated balloon."

Cloe glanced at Rome and again he shook his head. "He's probably in the shower," she lied.

"I don't hear the water running." There was a long pause and a definite smile was in Casey's voice when he spoke again. "No worries. I'm sure he'll show up eventually." He started whistling as his boot clicks faded.

"There are times I wish I was an only child," Rome grumbled before he looked at her. "So you're sure we're good?"

"I promise. We're good."

At least, she was. But in the days that followed, she realized Rome wasn't. After their morning of "release," he seemed to avoid her like the plague. He spent all day working the ranch. At meals, he took a seat on the other side of the table from her and let Casey do most of the talking. At night, he headed to his room with just a simple good night.

She should be relieved, but annoyed was a more accurate description of the way she felt. Extremely annoyed. He'd obviously thought things over and decided he couldn't chance the homely wall-flower falling in love with him by giving her any attention at all. The more he ignored her, the madder she got.

And the more projects she took on around the house to work out that anger.

She not only cooked breakfast and dinner, but she also made casseroles and baked pies and put them in the large freezer in the garage. She got the boxes she'd left at her parents' house that were filled with her things she'd packed when she'd moved out of her and Brandon's apartment and filled her room with knickknacks and pictures of her family and the quilt her mama's aunt had given her. She scrubbed down the porch and found three old rockers at a garage sale to put there. Today, she planned to make a garden in the front of the porch and fill it with the daffodils, tulips, and jonquils she'd gotten in town.

She had made friends with the animals. The dog, Blake Shelton, was lying in the dirt next to where she was hacking up the ground with a spade. The four barn cats, Tammy Wynette, Waylon Jennings, Reba McEntire, and George Jones—not to be confused with Decker and Sweetie's hound dog, George Strait—were napping on the porch in the sun. Mister Carson the goat was nosing around the flowers that were lined up on the porch steps. Cloe was about to issue a warning when Rome spoke behind her.

"What are you doing?"

She startled and glanced over her shoulder to see him standing there . . . looking like a sexy cowboy straight off the trail. A sexy cowboy she was extremely annoyed with. It had been much easier to keep her anger in check when Sam and Casey were there. But they had gone to Austin on business and wouldn't be back until tomorrow. Now that she and Rome were completely alone, she couldn't help being a little snide.

"What does it look like I'm doing? I'm getting ready to plant flowers. What are you doing?

I thought you said you wouldn't be back until late."

He didn't answer. His gaze seemed to be riveted to her butt. She figured it was covered in dirt. She reached behind her and brushed it off. "So why are you home so early?"

He jerked his attention away from her butt. "I ripped my jeans on a fence and need to change."

"Then change." She went back to hacking. When he didn't leave, she glanced over her shoulder. "Is there a problem?"

"I just don't understand why you're planting a garden when you're going to be leaving soon."

Talk about angry. She had to take two deep breaths to keep from exploding.

"I know I'm leaving, Rome. But I thought a little pop of color might be nice." She got up and his eyes seemed to widen. She was sure she looked silly in the gardening hat Casey had given her, but at the moment, she could have cared less. "But if you don't want flowers, you don't want flowers." She yanked off her gardening gloves and tossed them to the porch before she walked into the house, letting the screen door slam behind her.

She knew she was being irrational. He was right. Why would she plant flowers when she was only living there for a few months? Of course, she wasn't angry at him for questioning her flower planting. She was angry at him for ignoring her for the last few days. Even that was irrational, but she couldn't seem to help it.

Once in the bedroom, she realized how horrible she looked. Sweat and dirt streaked her cheeks and the floppy hat with its big pink gingham bow didn't help. She pulled it off and tossed it to the top of the dresser before she headed for the bathroom. She had just stripped down and stepped into the shower when the door opened and Rome walked in.

"Where did you get this?"

The glass door was fogged with steam, but she still tried to cover herself. "Get out!"

"Not until you tell me where you got this hat?"

She turned the shower off and reached her hand out the door for the towel that hung on the hook. Once it was wrapped securely around her, she stepped out of the shower. Rome stood there holding the gardening hat Casey had given her to use so she wouldn't get sunburned.

"Casey gave it to me and you can't just keep barging in on me while I'm showering."

"Then start locking the fucking door!"

She had never seen Rome this angry before, but she was just as angry. She stepped closer and got in his face. "I shouldn't have to lock the door when it's my door to my room! What were you doing in my room, anyway? I thought we were going to keep separate bedrooms so your wallflower wife wouldn't get too attached."

His eyes narrowed. "What are you talking about?"

"Don't play dumb, Rome. Not when you've ignored me ever since we had sex."

"It wasn't sex!"

"Fine! Ever since we reached orgasm together,

you have been acting like if you give me any kind of attention, I'm going to fall head over heels in love with you. News alert, Rome Remington. I'm not that stupid. I know what happened the other morning wasn't anything but sexual release and I haven't given it another thought." It was a lie. She had given it lots of thoughts. Which was probably another reason she was so angry.

"Well, good for you," he snapped. "Because I haven't been able to stop thinking about it."

She blinked. "What?"

His gaze lowered to where the towel was tucked in between her breasts. "That morning has haunted my every thought for the last three days." When he lifted his eyes, they were dark and smoky. "I wasn't avoiding you to save you, Cloe. I was avoiding you to save myself."

At his words, her anger melted away and all the feelings that had been hiding behind it consumed her. She knew she was going to get hurt. She knew it with every fiber of her being. But knowing didn't stop her from stepping closer and kissing him.

As soon as her lips touched his, he growled deep in his throat and jerked her close. At first, the kiss was desperate and frantic like they both couldn't get enough. But soon it slowed to a languid, drugging slide of lips and tongue that made Cloe's entire body feel like warm honey. When his hot, calloused hands slipped beneath the towel and cupped her butt cheeks, pressing her against his ridged fly, that honey turned to molten lava.

She moaned at the feel of hard man covered by

soft denim. He whispered against her lips. "Feel what you do to me, Lucky." He moved his hips, brushed his hard-on back and forth across the ache between her legs. "I've walked around for days like this. Wanting you and knowing that it will just make you leaving so much harder. But I can't resist you anymore."

He lifted her completely off her feet and set her on the counter between the double sinks. The granite was cold on her bare butt and her breath hitched, but he warmed her up quickly with another long, drugging kiss. As he kissed her, he untucked the towel and it slipped down around her hips. His hands nudged her legs apart and goose bumps rose as his calloused fingers caressed their way up her thighs and then slowly back down again. On the third trip, his fingers brushed over the juncture of her legs and she had to pull back from the kiss to catch her breath.

"You like that, Lucky?" he asked. She nodded and his eyes grew even hotter as he slipped between her folds and dipped one long finger inside her. "Me too. A lot. A whole hell of a lot."

He stroked her until she wiggled in frustration, then he pulled her closer to the edge and knelt between her legs. His intense gray gaze held her spellbound as he lowered his mouth. He watched her, gauging her every reaction until he found the tongue stroke and pace she liked the best. Then he set about giving her the best orgasm of her life.

Her eyes closed and her head fell back as wave after wave of pleasure washed over her. When it finally subsided, she opened her eyes to see him still kneeling in front of her with a look of wonder on his face. Like he had enjoyed it as much as she had. Of course, she realized that wasn't the case when he stood and she saw the bulge beneath his zipper.

She reached out and grabbed a belt loop, pulling him between her legs. It wasn't easy getting his straining zipper down and he ended up having to help. Once it was lowered, she eased the elastic waistband of his briefs down and released his hard length.

She took him in hand, stroking him until his hands gripped the counter on either side of her legs and his breath became rough and ragged. She would have liked to watch him orgasm, but he stopped her.

"I want to be in you. Is that okay?"

She nodded. "I want that too."

His smile was brilliant. He searched through two drawers until he found a box of condoms. Once he had one on, he returned to her. "We could go to the bed."

She shook her head. "I want you now."

His eyes dilated and he stepped closer, his hands gripping her butt. "I've wanted you since we woke up together in the hayloft."

She was surprised, but only for the second it took for him to slide deep inside her. Then all she could feel was the fulfilling stretch that fed an aching need she didn't even know she had until then. She tightened around him to keep him right where he was.

"Damn," he groaned. "You feel so good, Cloe."

He pulled out and thrust again. Even deeper this time. As he continued to thrust, his mouth dropped to her breast, his lips and tongue finding her nipple and sending showers of sensation rippling through her with each suck and lick. As he pumped harder and faster, his hand slipped between her legs to stroke her clit. She was stunned by how quickly that brought her to a second orgasm. As she moaned out her satisfaction, he reached orgasm with a string of guttural cusswords. Once it was over, his head dropped to her shoulder and she placed her arms around him and held him tightly.

Eventually, she would have to let him go.

But for now, nothing about this felt fake.

CHAPTER SIXTEEN

"IT WAS YOUR mother's gardening hat?" Cloe looked up at him with green eyes filled with tears. "Oh, Rome. I'm so sorry. I didn't know. Casey gave it to me. I just assumed it had been left by one of his many women."

Rome laughed. "I don't think he brings them home to garden." He picked up a strand of hair that had fallen across his chest. It slipped through his fingers like the curly ribbon on top of a Christmas present. Cloe had certainly turned out to be a present. One of the best presents he'd ever gotten. "And it doesn't matter if you borrow my mother's hat."

"Of course it matters," she said. "She's your mother. That hat is precious. In fact, it's too precious to be lying on the bathroom floor." She started to get up, but he pulled her back into his arms.

"It's okay, Cloe. I'll get it later." He was too comfortable now to move.

She snuggled back into his arms. "So your mama gardened?"

"That's the only memories I have of her, actually. She had a vegetable garden out back. She'd tell me nursery rhymes while she was working." He smiled at the memory. It surprised him. Memories of his mother had never made him happy before. But this one did. "She used to do different voices. Silly voices that made me laugh."

Cloe's fingers caressed the hair on his chest. "I bet she loves you."

He sighed. "Maybe. Just not enough to stay."

She hesitated. "Casey mentioned that she contacted you."

He continued to play with her hair. It was soothing and made his feelings much easier to get out. "I was a belligerent thirteen-year-old and told her to go to hell. Casey forgave her right away. He got the forgiveness gene I seem to be lacking. I wasn't willing to forgive Emily either when she called wanting closure."

"It's hard to forgive when you've been badly hurt."

He smiled. "Says the woman who I bet has no trouble forgiving. If Brandon called right this second and asked for forgiveness, what would you say?"

"I'd say, 'Sorry, Brandon, I don't have time to talk because I'm having amazing sex with my childhood sweetheart who has been crazy about me since kindergarten.'"

Rome didn't laugh. There was something about the sentence that struck him wrong. It wasn't the amazing part. What they'd shared *had* been amazing. It was the sex part. It hadn't felt like just sex. It had felt like so much more.

She tipped her head and looked at him. "I was kidding, Rome. I know you haven't been crazy about me since kindergarten."

He lost himself in the green of her eyes. "I should have been. I should've seen you for who you are."

She tipped her head. "And who is that?"

"A beautiful person. Inside and out." He kissed her.

This time, he took things slow as if he wanted to prove to her that whatever this was, it wasn't just sex. He worshiped her body with soft caresses and lingering kisses, reveling in each sigh and moan that came from her sweet lips. When she was breathless and begging, he entered her. Interlocking their fingers, he held her hands above her head and used deep, slow thrusts to bring them both to the edge. Their gazes held as they tumbled over together.

No, this wasn't sex.

But he wasn't willing to use another word.

Whatever it was, they spent the next week doing it whenever they got the chance. Rome made sure they got plenty of chances. He made excuses to come back to the house at all hours of the day. He forgot his hat. He needed to check on a horse in the stables. He needed to get his rain slicker—even though there wasn't a cloud in the sky. He was sure Daddy and Casey knew what he was doing, but, besides Casey's knowing smirk, they never said a word.

Cloe had completely won them over too.

Some of it was her cooking. Cloe's meals

were what country culinary dreams were made of. Before she had arrived, working past dinnertime had been no problem. The thought of Casey's cooking or a cold sandwich had not been enough to pull them away from herding cattle or mending fences. In fact, they'd paid no attention to time. Now, all three Remingtons had become clock-watchers. As soon as it got close to five o'clock—or even not so close—they finished up whatever they were working on and called it a day.

Sam and Casey didn't argue nearly as much as they had—of course, that was Cloe too. She had a calming effect on both men. If they started to get into it, she would step in and soften whatever harsh words had been spoken. "I'm sure Casey didn't mean any disrespect, Sam. He's very proud of all you've accomplished." "Like all fathers, your daddy just wants you to be all you can be, Casey."

Then there were times when she wasn't so soft. Like when all three of them had tracked in on her freshly mopped floors. After she had given them a thorough scolding, they now removed their boots, mud or no mud, in the mudroom. They also didn't wear their hats in the house. Nor did they dive into the succulent dishes she'd prepared until she'd taken a seat and said grace.

Rome loved her cooking as much as his brother and daddy. But that wasn't why he watched the clock, praying it would move faster. He thoroughly enjoyed dinner, but it was the time after dinner he enjoyed the most. Whether it was helping her do dishes and talking about their days, or sitting out on the front porch and enjoying the evening, or taking a walk down the country road and watching her excitement over all the spring wildflowers in bloom.

Or spending time in bed.

Cloe had a way of stripping off more than his clothes and making him feel comfortable in his own skin. When they were alone in bed, she seemed to feel the same way. In the last week, Rome had seen a side of her he'd never seen before. He realized how wrong he had been. Cloe Holiday was no wilting pansy. She was a steel magnolia. Under the soft-spoken façade was a strong, passionate woman who knew how to get her way without ever raising her voice.

She proved it Sunday morning when she woke him with a soft kiss. He went to pull her closer and deepen the kiss, but she drew away.

"No distractions this morning. I have to get ready for church."

"Church?"

She smiled. "Yes. You know the building in town with the tall steeple that's referred to as God's house. I promised Mimi I'd be there. You can come if you want. Your daddy and Casey are coming."

He stared at her. "You talked Sam and Casey into going to church? How did you manage that?"

"I just told them how much it would mean to me if we attended as a family."

Family. There was something about the word that made his heart tighten.

Since Rome was a little boy, his daddy had stressed the importance of family. He'd taught Rome that blood was thicker than water. That your lineage and where you came from mattered. And keeping that lineage going was what mattered the most. Rome had believed him. He'd worked hard all his life to uphold the Remington name and to grow the ranch and make it bigger and better. But now, he realized family wasn't about lineage or a ranch. It was about people. Not just people who had your same blood, but people who came into your life and made it better.

Cloe had made his life better.

Except she wasn't his family. This was all a ruse that would end as soon as Mimi paid off the loan and signed over the land.

"Rome?"

He pulled out of his thoughts and found Cloe looking at him with concern.

"Are you okay?"

He forced a smile. "I'm fine. We better hurry or we'll be late for church." ·

He didn't talk much on the ride into town. Thankfully, no one seemed to notice since Casey was taking a poll to see who thought lightning would strike the church as soon as the Remingtons crossed the threshold.

"Which is why you're going first, Romy," Casey said. "If it does strike, I'm outta there."

"Stop, Casey," Cloe said. "Can't you see you're freaking your brother out?"

Rome was feeling freaked out, but it had nothing to do with lightning and everything to do with the realization that he was doing it again. He was falling for a woman who would eventually leave. He needed to put on the brakes and get back their previous relationship—two business partners making a logical decision. But when they got to church and she slipped her hand in his and this feeling of contentment washed over him, he knew there was no going back.

It scared the hell out of him.

Inside the church, Mrs. Stokes was the first person to greet them. "Well, it's about time you lovebirds showed up."

Casey mumbled under his breath to Rome. "I'd rather have been hit by lightning."

"What was that, Casey Remington?" Mrs. Stokes started coughing.

Casey pulled off his hat and waited until the fit was over before he spoke. "I was just telling my brother how time hasn't changed your beauty, Ms. Stokes."

She waved a hand. "Don't be wasting that charm on me. Everyone knows I don't date men under forty years of age." She winked at Sam. "I like my men like I like my wine and cheese. Aged."

Casey crowed with laughter and Mrs. Stokes swatted him. "Hush up! That's no way to act in church." She slipped her wrinkled hand through the crook of his arm. "Now walk me to my pew. I'd invite y'all to join me, but I figure you'll be sittin' in the Holiday family pew."

Family. There was that word again tightening Rome's chest and making him feel like he couldn't breathe.

He allowed Cloe to lead him down the aisle to the Holiday pew. Her grandmother, mama, and daddy were already seated. Rome didn't know who glared the most—Hank or Sam. Sam stubbornly took a seat in the pew behind the Holidays'.

Cloe started to say something, but Rome shook his head and stopped her. It was best if they kept their fathers separated. Especially in church. But Casey had no problem joining the Holiday family. He took a seat right next to Mimi and started chatting away. Rome allowed Cloe to go into the pew before him, then took a seat next to her.

All through church, he tried to absorb the fact that he'd been completely wrong. He thought he could keep his distance from Cloe. He thought he could remain detached. But he *was* attached. In only a few weeks, he'd become tethered to the woman sitting next to him holding his hand as if she never wanted to let it go.

But Emily had held his hand like that too. And she'd let go. His and Emily's had been a real marriage. His and Cloe's had been fake from the start.

"If you're uncomfortable, we can leave."

Cloe's voice pulled him from his thoughts and he glanced over to see her watching him with concerned eyes.

He tightened his hold on her hand. "I'm fine."

But he wasn't. He wasn't fine at all.

After church, Mimi cornered him in the foyer. Her eyes were twinkling and her smile was big. He'd never noticed before, but underneath the wrinkles were dimples just like Cloe's.

"I'm ready to transfer the ranch into your name."

A stab of pain pierced his heart. "I thought you wanted to wait a few months to see if Cloe and I made a good match."

"I was never worried about you making a good match. I was worried about you getting divorced before you figured out that you made a good match. But according to what your brother just told me, you have figured it out. He said love is in the air at Remington Ranch." She patted his cheek. "I guess my plan wasn't as crazy as everyone thought."

It was still a crazy plan, but what was even crazier was Rome thinking he could live with a woman as beautiful, smart, caring, and wonderful as Cloe and not fall completely under her spell.

But Casey was wrong. It wasn't love. Mutual respect, definitely. Lust, most definitely. But not love.

Darla Holiday walked up. "I hope you're telling Rome about our plan for a surprise birthday party for Cloe on Friday."

Cloe's birthday was this coming Friday? She hadn't said a word. Of course, that wasn't her style. She didn't like drawing attention to herself. She didn't want people doing things for her as much as she wanted to do things for other people.

His gaze searched for her and he found her talking to her father by the open doors of the church. She noticed him watching her and a smile softened her face. His breath got caught in his lungs and his heart felt like it was beating out of his chest. All his denials melted away beneath those pretty green eyes.

He knew.

He knew that no matter how much he denied it, it was too late to worry about falling.

He'd already fallen.

He didn't remember driving home from church. Nor did he remember the excuse he gave for not going inside with everyone else to eat the dinner Cloe had put in the Crock-Pot that morning. Instead, he headed to the stables and saddled up his horse. He rode long and hard, trying to outrun the fear gnawing at his gut. Fear that he was headed for the same heartache he'd felt when his mother and then Emily had left.

But he couldn't outrun the pain. Soon he slowed his horse and just accepted that it was too late. His heart was going to break again.

His cellphone rang. It was probably Cloe wondering if he was okay. As much as he didn't feel like talking to her, he couldn't let her worry. He pulled his cellphone from his pocket. But it wasn't Cloe. It was his lawyer. He answered, curious as to why she was calling on a Sunday.

"I hate to bother you on a Sunday, Rome, but I've been out of town on business and just discovered this report on my desk and figured you'd want this information as soon as possible." There was the sound of paper shuffling. "You know how you asked me to find out as much as I could about Oleander Investments? Well, while I was away, my assistant discovered that it's owned by Corbin Whitlock."

"Corbin Whitlock? That name sounds familiar."

"It should. He lived in Wilder for a while. My assistant also found out that Oleander Investments have filed a foreclosure lawsuit and is claiming ownership of the Holiday Ranch."

CHAPTER SEVENTEEN

"SO WHAT HAPPENED from Sunday at church to now to take that sparkle from your eyes?"

Cloe glanced over at her grandmother. Mimi had arrived that morning loaded down with gifts. There was a tea set that was Cloe's great-great grandmother's and an entire car trunk of flowers Mimi had taken from her own garden.

She and Mimi were planting those flowers now. Mimi in a wide-brimmed gardening hat and Cloe wearing one of Rome's old cowboy hats. She had carefully wrapped and boxed Rome's mother's gardening hat and placed it in a sealable, plastic bin before finding a spot for it on the top shelf of the closet.

"I'm guessing you and Rome had a fight," Mimi said. "But there's no need to fret. An occasional spat is just part of marriage."

Cloe wished it was just a spat. But it was far more than that. Rome had slept in the spare room last night. He claimed it was because he had business to take care of in Houston and needed to get up early and didn't want to wake her, but she knew that wasn't the case. She knew his sudden cold shoulder had nothing to do with ranch work and waking her and everything to do with him realizing that they had gotten too close.

He was right.

They had gotten too close. Or, at least, she had gotten too close to him. Before when he had ignored her, she'd just felt annoyed and angry. Now, she felt like her heart had been dug out of her chest and was lying naked and exposed—just like the tulip bulbs her grandmother was getting ready to replant.

And it wasn't just Rome she had gotten attached to. Casey had become the ornery little brother she'd never had and Sam was a good man who struggled to show his emotions—just like her own daddy. They had started to feel like family. Remington Ranch had started to feel like home.

She loved cooking and baking in the kitchen and gardening in the garden and going out to the barn to see Blake and the country music cats. She loved riding Lady Grantham every day and had started thinking about starting a vegetable garden in the spot on the other side of the stables and putting up a chicken coop.

She had started believing this was all real.

No wonder Rome had withdrawn. He had seen what was happening and didn't want her to get hurt.

But it was too late for that.

She was already hurt.

And it wasn't Rome's fault. It was hers. He had

been completely upfront with her. She knew how he felt about love and marriage. She had entered into this relationship knowing it was all just a ruse. If it was no longer a ruse to her, that was her problem. Not Rome's. She needed to pull her head out of the clouds and accept the fact that this wasn't her home. Casey and Sam weren't her family. And Rome wasn't ever going to fall in love with her.

Ever.

She carefully picked up the tulip bulbs and placed them in the hole she'd dug. As she covered them up with dirt, she tried to bury her own feelings. "Rome and I didn't get in a fight," she said. "I'm just not feeling very well today." It was the truth. Her stomach had been upset all morning. No doubt related to the ache in her chest.

"Well, why didn't you say something before?" Mimi got to her feet. "You don't need to be out in this hot sun if you aren't feeling well. Let's go inside and I'll make you some tea with honey."

Mimi made them tea while Cloe put what was left of the coffee cake she'd made for breakfast on a plate for her grandmother. Casey had devoured most of the cake. For having not an ounce of fat on him, the man could put away the baked goods.

"This is as good as your mama's," Mimi said as soon as she took a bite of the coffee cake. "And I thought you didn't like to bake."

"I like to bake and cook. I just never had the opportunity before. Brandon didn't eat sweets because of the calories and it seemed a shame to only bake for myself."

"You could have helped your mama cook when you lived at home."

"Noelle always wanted to help Mama. I didn't want to get in the way of her passion."

Mimi set down her fork and studied her. "Just because Noelle loves cooking didn't mean you couldn't have joined in baking with her and your mama. I get it. You adore your sisters and have always stepped back in their shadows so they could have their moment in the sun. But you need to step up and get your moment in the sun too." She glanced around. "And it looks like you finally have. I've never seen you shine so brightly than when you walked into that church with Rome. Confidence radiated out of you like sunshine bursting out from the clouds. A good man can do that for a woman—make her realize her worth. Just like a good woman can do that for a man. Casey said Rome is happier than he's ever been."

Cloe couldn't help the tears that filled her eyes. She looked away, but it was too late. Her grandmother took her hand.

"Tell me what's going on, Clover Fields."

Unable to keep her secret any longer, she turned to her grandmother. "My marriage is fake, Mimi. Rome and I never planned to stay married."

Mimi studied her for only a second before she burst out laughing.

Cloe stared at her. "I'm not kidding."

Mimi sobered. "I knew all along you didn't marry Rome because you loved him. You married him because you love me."

"You knew?"

"Of course I knew. Everyone in town knows why you two got hitched. According to Fiona, they started a betting pool on when you'll get divorced."

"Then if you knew, why didn't you say so instead of forcing Rome to wait to get your land?"

"Because I was hoping for exactly what happened. I was hoping that you'd fall in love."

She shook her head. "I don't love Rome, Mimi." Just to make sure her heart had heard, she repeated herself. "I don't love—"

A noise from the mudroom cut her off. She got up to investigate when Rome stepped into the kitchen. Because he'd been in Houston, he wasn't dressed in his usual ranch clothes. He wore a pressed western shirt and jeans and his good boots and Stetson.

His gaze held hers for a second before he took off his hat and looked at Mimi. "Hey, Ms. Mimi. I didn't realize you were coming for a visit."

"I figured since it's been over two weeks that your honeymoon is over. At least figuratively." Cloe blushed as her grandmother continued. "So Hank's going to set up a meeting with Oleander Investments this week to pay off the loan. I figure I can sign the ranch over as soon as we have the deed."

A look passed over Rome's face. A resigned look that instantly made Cloe wary. "I wish it was that simple, Ms. Mimi. Did you get a registered letter from Oleander Investments a good six months ago?"

Mimi's eyes crinkled at the corners. "Was it six months ago? I can't remember exactly, but I got a letter."

Cloe turned to her grandmother. "You never told me about a registered letter."

"Because it wasn't important. They were just wanting their money and we didn't have it."

Rome sighed and ran a hand through his hair. "They weren't just wanting their money. They were letting you know that you had gone for-ty-five days without a payment and if you didn't pay them in full immediately, they were going to foreclose on your property." He hesitated. "Which they have started the proceedings to do."

Cloe stared at him. "But you're going to pay them in full."

He sighed. "Unfortunately, the contract has already been breached."

"So you're saying there's no way to stop the foreclosure?"

Before he could answer, Mimi jumped in. "Of course, there's a way. Rome can pay off the loan."

"That might have worked if you had taken the loan out at Wilder bank. Mrs. Stokes owns the bank and would have given you some leeway. A big company won't."

"But they might," Cloe said. "At least we can ask them."

Rome looked defeated and Cloe knew what he was going to say before he said it. "I met with the loan manager of Oleander Investments today and they are not willing to stop the foreclosure proceedings. As far as they're concerned, the Holiday Ranch—including the house and barn that is included in the title—is now theirs."

As Cloe stared at Rome in disbelief, Mimi spoke. "Bull hockey! The Holiday Ranch has been in my family for over a century. Some big company can't just come along and take it."

"I'm afraid they can, Ms. Mimi. Both my lawyer and I have read through the contract carefully. There's no way to dispute it."

Mimi jumped to her feet, her face red and her hands trembling. "But I won't allow it! Do you hear me? That's Holiday land and it will stay—" She cut off suddenly and all the color drained from her face.

Then she collapsed.

"Mimi!" Cloe screamed as she rushed over to catch her. Rome beat her to it and carefully lowered her to the floor.

"Call 911," he said as he checked her pulse.

Mimi regained consciousness as Cloe was making the call, but still seemed disoriented. Cloe couldn't blame her. She was feeling disoriented too. By the time the paramedics arrived, Mimi was more coherent and wanted nothing to do with going to the hospital, but the paramedics thought it was a good idea to have her checked out by a doctor.

Cloe rode with her in the ambulance and she ranted the entire ride about how no one was going to take her ranch. Once at the county hospital, the doctor ordered some tests run, and afterward, they put Mimi in a room to await the results. Mama and Daddy arrived. When Cloe explained what had caused Mimi to collapse, she worried her father would collapse too. Or worse, have another heart attack.

But he took it much calmer than Mimi had.

"If it's done, it's done. There's nothing we can do about it now."

It was almost ten o'clock at night when they finally wheeled Mimi toward the sliding doors that led out to the parking lot. When they passed the waiting room, Cloe was shocked to see Rome sitting there with his arms resting on his knees and his head in his hands.

"Rome?"

He glanced up, then quickly got to his feet and looked at her grandmother. "How are you, Ms. Mimi?"

Cloe worried her grandmother would start ranting again, but she seemed to be all ranted out. "I've had better days."

Rome nodded. "I'm sorry. I shouldn't have broken the news so bluntly."

Mimi flapped a hand. "There's no hiding from the truth. It's my fault for not getting my reading glasses and reading that letter more carefully. And don't you worry. You'll get your land. I'm not through fighting yet."

"Yes, you are, Mama," Daddy said. "At least for tonight." He nodded at Rome before he rolled the wheelchair toward the sliding doors.

Mama gave Cloe a hug. "I'll keep you posted on how she's doing." She hugged Rome and whispered something in his ear that made him nod before she followed after Daddy and Mimi.

Cloe wished she could go home with her family and not have to deal with the aftermath of the ranch being foreclosed on. But like her grandmother had said. *There's no hiding from the truth.* The truth was now that the Holidays were losing the ranch, there was no need for Cloe and Rome to stay in a pretend marriage.

Rome knew it too.

"I guess we have some things we need to talk about."

She nodded, unsure if she could speak around the lump in her throat. They walked out to his truck in silence. As always, he opened her door and held out his hand to help her in. But this time, she refused to take it. She couldn't touch him.

Not now.

Not ever again.

Once they were heading back to Wilder, she finally got a hold of her emotions enough so she could speak.

"This didn't turn out exactly how we had planned, did it?"

"No." His voice sounded tight and forced. She knew this wasn't easy for him either. He had never set out to hurt her. And yet, there she sat more hurt than she had ever felt in her life.

But she didn't have to let him know that.

"I'll move out tomorrow. There's no need to come up with a story to tell everyone. According to Mimi, everyone in town knows why we got married and are taking bets on when we're getting a divorce. I guess Mrs. Stokes had this week." She forced a laugh, but it came out sounding nothing like a laugh. "After all her relationships and marriages, the woman obviously knows when two people aren't going to work."

She waited for him to say something. But he didn't say a word. He just stared straight ahead with one hand on the steering wheel and the other fisted on the console between them. She knew he was struggling to find words that would make her feel better. That broke her heart even more.

"It's fine, Rome. My family will be fine and I'm fine. I know you thought I was getting too attached. But I never thought it was more than it was. I knew this was only a business proposition. Yes, we might have crossed a line we shouldn't have crossed, but we're adults. There was no harm done."

Again, he didn't say a word. And she was completely out of them. So she joined him in the silence and stared out the windshield.

When they got back to the house, she didn't wait for him to open her door. As soon as he finished pulling into the garage, she got out and went inside. Casey and Sam had already gone to bed. She made her way up the stairs to her room. Behind her, she could hear the clicks of Rome's boots. Why the sound seemed so lonely, she didn't know. She hesitated by her door. She didn't know what she hoped for . . . a word . . .

a touch . . . any sign that something about what they'd shared had been real.

But all she got was the sound of Rome walking past her.

CHAPTER EIGHTEEN

"FIONA STOKES IS claiming she won the betting pool." Melba shifted the overweight pug in her arms. "But as I have pointed out repeatedly, nothing is official until the divorce papers are signed and that takes at least ninety days. It took Jep and me an entire year. Of course, he fought over everything. Cloe doesn't seem like the fighting kind."

At Melba's words, the heartache Rome had been struggling with for the last few days came back with a vengeance. No, Cloe wasn't the fighting kind. She certainly hadn't fought for him. She hadn't shed one tear or given one damn about leaving him.

All the way back from Houston, a glimmer of hope had remained in his heart—hope that what he had with Cloe was more than just a business arrangement. Then he had walked into the house and overheard her words to her grandmother and that hope had died a quick death.

I don't love Rome.

He had thought he'd been hurt when Emily

left. It didn't compare to what he'd felt when he heard Cloe speak those words. But he'd gotten through two women he loved leaving him. He'd get through this.

He poured himself another shot of tequila and downed it while Melba set the pug on the bar. The fat pug waddled over to Rome and enthusiastically licked him in the face.

"Would you look at that," Melba said. "Buck Owens loves you already. And did I mention that he's smart as a whip and completely housebroke?"

Rome scratched the dog's ears. "Did I mention that I don't want another dog?"

She sighed. "Okay. I'll let you off the hook this time, but only because you're obviously upset over losing—"

"I'm not upset over losing Cloe Holiday!" he snapped much more harshly than he'd intended.

Buck Owens cowered and hurried back to Melba who was looking at Rome as if he'd just sprouted horns. "I wasn't going to say Cloe," she said. "I was going to say the Holiday Ranch. The entire town has known all along why you two got married. You two couldn't be a more unlikely couple." She paused and studied him intently. "But maybe we've all been wrong."

"You weren't wrong. Cloe and I are complete opposites. The only reason I married her was for her family's ranch."

"Bullshit!"

Rome glanced up to see Casey standing there with the same scowl he'd been wearing for the last two days. After Cloe left, Casey had refused to talk to him. Obviously, the silent treatment was over.

"You might have only married her to get her land, but losing the land isn't why you're sitting here drinking tequila. You screwed up and you know it. Instead of stopping her and telling her how you feel, you let her walk out the door and didn't do a damn thing to stop her. And she wanted you to. Her eyes were begging you to."

"She wasn't begging me for anything but to let her leave without some big scene." Rome glanced around at the people who had stopped talking and were obviously listening in. "And speaking of making a scene."

Casey shook his head. "You learned so well from Daddy. Remingtons shouldn't make big scenes. We have our family name to uphold. If bad things happen, we should just grin and bear it." He forced a laugh. "And look where that got us. Three lonely bachelors living miserably together."

"If you don't like living with me and Daddy, you can always move out."

"After what you did to Cloe, I'm damn well thinking about it. But before I go, I'm going to knock some sense into that stubborn head of yours. There are times to make scenes, Rome. And one of those times is when the woman you love walks out the door."

"I don't love Cloe." He poured another shot of tequila and downed it. The burning helped him accept the lie.

"The hell you don't. I saw you two together.

I always questioned your love for Emily. But I never questioned your love for Cloe."

"It certainly looked like love to me." Mrs. Stokes stepped up to the bar. "And believe me, after all my relationships, I know love when I see it." She waved at the bartender. "Give me my usual, Smithy."

"If you thought it was love, Fiona," Melba said. "Why did you join the betting pool?"

"I put my money in before I saw them together. At church, Rome had that deer-caught-in-the-headlights look men get when they've figured out they can't live without a woman."

"That's it, isn't it?" Casey stared at Rome. "You're running scared. You love her and you'd rather let her go than find out she doesn't love you."

Rome's temper snapped. "She doesn't love me! I heard her say so herself."

Casey looked stunned. "She told you she didn't love you?"

"No. She told her grandmother and I overheard."

"Maybe she's in denial too," Mrs. Stokes said. "Mimi told me all about Cloe's break up with her boyfriend. She gave the idiot six long years of her life and he screwed her over good. That can make a woman scared to declare her love again. Did you even ask her to stay?"

"I'm not going to force someone to stay when they want to leave."

Casey snorted. "Of course you're not. Daddy did the same thing and look how that turned out.

Is that what you want for yourself? To be a bitter man all alone like Daddy? Don't let that happen, Romy. Accept that you love Cloe."

"Fine! I love Cloe. Is that supposed to make me feel better? Because it doesn't."

"It might if you tell her," Melba said.

He shook his head. "That would be a no."

"Then I guess I won the betting pool." Mrs. Stokes picked up her whiskey and left.

"She didn't win," Melba said. "It's not final until the ink dries on the divorce papers. That puts me in the running." She glanced down the bar and a big smile spread over her face. "Hey! How's Taylor Swift doing?"

Rome followed her gaze to a cowboy sitting at the other end of the bar. His Stetson was pulled too low to be able to see his features, but his voice sounded familiar when he spoke.

"I thought you said the kitten was sweet natured. I have scratches to prove otherwise."

Melba laughed. "Tay-Tay does have a sweet nature. But just like Taylor Swift, she also has a little bit of sass." She glanced down at the pug that had fallen asleep in her arms. "What she needs is a friend to keep her company."

The cowboy held up his hands. "Nope. You hoodwinked me once. I'm not falling for it again."

"Oh, come on, Corbin Whitlock," Melba said. "Buck Owens and Taylor Swift are bound to be good friends.

It took Rome's tequila-soaked brain a few minutes to catch up. When it did, he stiffened. "Did you say Corbin Whitlock?"

"I sure did." Melba shifted Buck Owens to her other arm. "You remember him, don't ya? He and his little sister lived here with their uncle, Dan Wheeler, for a short time." She shook her head. "Poor kids. That man was a mean drunk if ever there was one. Corbin seemed to be just the opposite. Very polite and mannerly. Taylor Swift took right to him. You can always tell a good person by how animals react to them."

"He's not a good person." Rome got to his feet. He'd been looking for a way to release some of his frustrations. He figured he'd just found it.

Casey must have read the anger on Rome's face because he followed after him. "What's going on, Rome? You know this Corbin guy?"

Corbin hadn't been at the meeting Rome and his lawyer had with Oleander Investments' loan manager. So when he tapped him on the shoulder and Corbin swiveled on his barstool, Rome didn't recognize the face under the cowboy hat. But Corbin recognized him and Casey.

"Well, if it isn't the Remingtons." Corbin pushed back his cowboy hat and smiled a smile that didn't reach his eyes. "I guess by the look on your face that things are about to get ugly."

"Damn right they are." Rome drew back his fist and punched Corbin, knocking him off his barstool. He went for him again, but this time, Corbin was ready. He ducked and punched Rome in the stomach. It caused him to suck wind, but he rallied quickly and landed a right to Corbin's face that had him falling back against the bar and knocking over his glass of beer.

The bouncers arrived and when they tried to grab Rome, Casey joined the fight. But two Remingtons were no match for six burly bouncers. Soon, they were both pinned face first to the sticky bar floor. When Decker arrived, he didn't look happy about being called away from his bed the first night he was back in Wilder after his honeymoon. Surprisingly, Corbin didn't press charges. And since the only damage was a broken beer glass, Bobby Jay didn't either. But that didn't stop Decker from being pissed.

"So let me get this straight," he said once they were standing out in the parking lot. "You punched the owner of the investment company that holds the title to the Holiday Ranch. So pretty much any chance we had of reasoning with him and getting him to stop the foreclosure is now gone."

Decker was right. Rome had screwed up. He had screwed up badly. "I'm sorry. When I heard his name, I just lost it."

Decker blew out his breath. "I can't believe he's foreclosing on the Holiday Ranch. I had a math class with him in high school. He seemed like a nice enough guy—kept to himself and never caused trouble."

"Well, he's making up for it now," Casey said. "If I had known who he was, I would have punched him myself."

"Hotheadedness isn't going to fix this," Decker said. "I figure I'll give him a day or two and then go see him. Maybe I can talk him out of fore closing on the ranch if you pay off the Holidays' debt."

Rome wished it was that easy. "I don't know if that's still possible."

"What do you mean?"

Casey jumped in. "What he means is that Cloe and Rome split up and Mimi might not be willing to sign over the land to a man who broke her granddaughter's heart."

"I didn't break her heart, Casey."

Casey rolled his eyes. "You are so damn blind where woman are concerned, Rome. You thought Emily loved you and it was as plain as the nose on my face that she was just in love with the thought of being married to a wealthy Texas rancher. Now you think Cloe was only interested in your money and paying off her family's loan. But if that's the case, then why did she work so hard to make the ranch a home. Her home." He waved a hand. "But go ahead and keep your head in the sand and let her get away. I'm done trying to get through that thick skull of yours." He turned and headed for his truck.

When he was gone, Decker looked at Rome. "I really hope Casey's not right. If you broke Cloe's heart, my wife is going to come after you just like you went after Corbin." He paused. "And I won't stop her."

Rome didn't care if Sweetie beat him up. She couldn't make him feel more bruised than he already did. All the way back to the ranch, all he could think about were Casey's words. When his headlights flashed over the front of the house as he pulled in, he realized Casey was right.

Cloe had made the house a home.

At one time, it had just been a plain stone building with no color whatsoever. Now the shutters on the living room and kitchen windows were painted a bright blue. On the porch, two lemon-yellow rocking chairs sat with daisy-print pillows. Rome had sat in those chairs, but he'd never given any thought to where she had found them or how much work it had taken to paint them and the shutters. Or to cultivate and plant the garden in a brilliant rainbow of spring flowers.

All of those things had taken time. As did cooking meals and baking pies.

Cloe hadn't had to do any of it. She could have spent all her time with her family at their house. Instead, she worked hard to make this house as homey as her own.

Why?

Confused, he pulled into the garage and headed into the house. In the kitchen, he pulled a bag of frozen corn out of the freezer and placed it on his jaw as he made his way to the stairs. He stopped when he saw the flickering light coming from his father's study. When he peeked in the open door, he saw Sam sitting in front of a crackling fire staring into the flames.

"Hey, Dad."

Sam startled and glanced over his shoulder at Rome. "I didn't hear you come in." His gaze lowered to the bag of corn Rome was holding to his jaw. "Casey told me what happened."

Rome moved to the chair by the fire and sat down. "I guess you're pissed at us for causing a scene."

"There are good reasons to cause a scene. Sounds like you had one."

"I thought you'd be happy the Holidays are losing their ranch."

Sam hesitated before he spoke. "Maybe it's time I gave up that grudge."

Rome was surprised, but he shouldn't be. It looked like he wasn't the only one who had fallen for Cloe. They both stared at the fire for a long time before Sam spoke.

"So she's not coming back?"

It was hard to get the words out. "I don't think so."

There was a long pause before his father spoke. "I'm sorry, son."

The words held sincerity and pain. If anyone knew how he felt, Rome figured his father did. He couldn't help asking the question he'd always been too afraid to ask. "Why did Mama leave, Daddy? I know she was unhappy, but why was she unhappy?" He hesitated. "Was it me?"

Sam turned to him with surprise. "Of course it wasn't you. Your mama left for a lot of reasons, but none of them had to do with you. You were just a kid. She left because of me." He looked back at the fire. "She left because I couldn't give her what every woman deserves—unconditional love."

Rome stared at his father's strong profile. "You didn't love her?"

Sam heaved a deep sigh. "I loved her . . . just not as much as I loved someone else."

"You were in love with someone else? Who?"

"It doesn't matter. What matters is that your mother found out and felt like she would always be my second choice. Probably because that was how I treated her." He shook his head. "I was wrong. I should have been thankful for what I had, instead of longing for what I didn't." He glanced at Rome. "And maybe I was wrong to fight so hard to get full custody of you boys. I used every powerful connection I had and hired the best lawyers I could find to keep you boys here on the ranch with me. That was selfish. I should have let you spend time with your mama."

"She could have fought for that time too, Daddy, and she didn't."

"People make mistakes, Rome. She called and tried to fix that mistake. You wouldn't let her."

It was true. He had refused to even talk to his mom. He'd done the same thing to Emily. She was the one in the wrong—the one who had given up—so she could just go to hell. But now he realized that there were two sides to every story. Both his mother and Emily had their sides. He had to wonder if they were as similar as his and his father's. Sam hadn't loved Glorieta enough and Rome hadn't loved Emily enough either. He had married her because that's what Sam had wanted him to do. But she had always come second to the ranch.

He'd proven that by letting her go without a fight.

Just like his father had done with his mother.

And just like his mother had done with Rome and Casey.

If you love someone—truly love them—you never give up on them. You go after them and do whatever you have to do to keep them.

He got up and headed for the door.

"Where are you going?" his father asked.

"To figure out how to get my wife back."

CHAPTER NINETEEN

NO ONE SAID a word to Cloe about moving back home. The one time Daddy mentioned Rome, Mama gave him a look that shut him up in a hurry. Cloe was thankful. Just the mention of Rome's name brought tears to her eyes and a shaft of pain to her heart. She had thought she was upset when Brandon had broken up with her, but that pain was nothing compared to the pain she lived with now.

Mimi seemed to know Cloe needed something to keep her mind occupied. The morning after she moved back, she plopped one of her gardening hats on her head and pushed her outside to help plant the vegetable garden. They'd spent the last week working side by side in the fertile earth planting lettuce, tomatoes, green beans, corn, squash, cucumbers, carrots, peas, beets, peppers, okra, and pumpkins—even though they probably wouldn't be there to reap the rewards.

On Friday, Sweetie came over. All her sisters knew what had happened. Like everyone else, they were upset about losing the ranch, but steered away from the subject of Rome and Cloe.

Sweetie didn't mention Rome either, but she did pull Cloe into her arms and hold her much longer than usual.

"You okay, Clo?"

Cloe pushed back the tears and nodded against her shoulder. "I'm fine. It was a fake marriage, after all."

But there was nothing fake about Sweetie's marriage. She looked happier than Cloe had ever seen her. Once they were seated in the living room with Mama and Mimi, she talked nonstop about everything she and Decker had done while they were in Nashville. Not only the sightseeing, but also the meeting she'd had with the executives of a large recording company that wanted to buy some of the songs Sweetie had written.

"They're going to buy twenty-three of them." Sweetie beamed with pride. As depressed as she felt, Cloe couldn't help being happy for her sister. She knew how hard Sweetie had worked to achieve her dream of succeeding in the music business.

"But enough about Nashville," Sweetie said as she opened the huge photo album she'd brought. "I brought the wedding pictures and I can't wait for y'all to see them."

The wedding photographs had turned out great. The big red barn was the perfect backdrop for Sweetie in their mama's wedding dress and Decker in his western tux.

"And wait until you see the group pictures," Sweetie said as she flipped to the photographs of the wedding party.

Cloe's heart tightened. Rome looked breath-takingly handsome in his tuxedo and Stetson. For once in her life, Cloe didn't look like a pale ghost with a forced smile. Her cheeks were flushed and her eyes twinkled and her smile actually looked real. In one photograph, she was out-and-out laughing. Rome wasn't looking at the camera in that picture. He was looking at her, his hand on her waist and his head bent so that his cowboy hat shaded her face.

They looked like a couple.

A couple in love.

Just that quickly tears sprang to Cloe's eyes. A few escaped and trickled down her cheek before she quickly brushed them away. She thought no one had noticed. But as soon as they were through looking at the album, Sweetie got up from the couch and held out her hand to Cloe.

"Come on, Clo. Let's go out on the porch and catch up."

The entire front porch was decorated for St. Patrick's Day, which had been yesterday. Lepre-chauns holding pots of gold peeked out of the flowers in the garden. Green ribbon wrapped around the porch bannister and railing. And a large wreath filled with glittery shamrocks and little leprechauns' hats hung from the door.

"Looks like Mama is not letting the sale of the ranch keep her from her holiday decorating," Sweetie said as they took a seat in the swing.

"I don't think anything will keep her from that," Cloe said. "I'm hoping we'll be able to find us a place to live with a front porch. Even a small one."

Sweetie glanced at her. "Us?"

Cloe nodded. "I'm staying in Wilder. I can't leave Mama, Daddy, and Mimi when they're about to lose everything."

"They will never lose everything. They'll always have us." Sweetie set the swing to swaying. "And what about you and Rome?"

"There is no me and Rome. There never was. It was all a business proposition. The only reason we were together was for him to get the land and me to save the house. Now that Corbin has started foreclosure proceedings, there's no reason for us to stay married."

Sweetie smiled sadly. "That certainly makes sense if you and Rome were just business part-ners. But I don't think that's what you were, Cloe. I think you were much more to each other. Even before you got married."

"There was nothing between me and Rome before we got married."

"My wedding pictures say differently. There was something between you two even then. A spark of interest. Physical attraction. Whatever you want to call it. Photographs don't lie."

"Maybe we just felt comfortable with each other."

Sweetie stopped pushing the swing and her gaze pinned her. "Just how comfortable did you get with Rome?" When Cloe's cheeks heated, her eyes widened. "You had sex?"

"It didn't mean anything. It was just something that happened."

"It just happened? You don't ever let things just happen. You plan out everything. You didn't have sex with Brandon until you'd been dating for close to two years."

It was the truth. She'd planned out the night she'd had sex with Brandon from birth control to the thread count of the sheets. But with Rome, she hadn't thought about anything . . . but being in his arms. He had that kind of power over her. The kind that completely obliterated logical, levelheaded plans.

Tears welled in her eyes again. This time, she didn't try to stop them. "I fell in love with him, Sweetie. I knew he couldn't love me back—didn't want to love me back—and I still fell in love with him."

"Oh, Clo." Sweetie pulled her into her arms and held her close. "I know. Believe me, I know. I didn't want to fall for Decker either. We were the complete opposites—lived in completely different towns. Not to mention, he was Jace's cousin. But love isn't something you can plan. It just happens. Are you sure Rome doesn't feel the same way?"

Cloe nodded her head against Sweetie's shoulder. "After his mama and first wife left him, he doesn't believe in love anymore."

"He doesn't believe or he's just scared?"

"Both."

Sweetie huffed. "Men! I swear they can take an extremely simple thing and make it complicated."

Cloe lifted her head and wiped at her cheeks. "And we don't?"

Sweetie laughed. "Point taken. But with love, it's usually the guy who has all the fears." She sent Cloe a look. "And it's usually us that have to get them over those fears."

Cloe wished it were that simple. "He doesn't love me, Sweetie. I could feel him starting to pull away from me as soon as we started getting too serious."

"Maybe he wasn't just worried about you getting hurt, Cloe. Maybe he was also worried about himself."

Sweetie's words reminded her of the words Rome had spoken to her right before they'd made love the first time. *I wasn't avoiding you to save you, Cloe. I was avoiding you to save myself.* What if Sweetie was right? What if his avoidance hadn't been because Cloe was getting too close? It was because he was?

She shook her head. "It still doesn't matter. If Rome's not willing to give love a chance, it could never work between us."

Sweetie sighed and pulled her back into her arms. "I'm so sorry, Cloe. I wish you had never married Rome."

Cloe could have easily stayed in her sister's arms and wallowed in self-pity. But she knew that wouldn't do her any good. She might not be the most beautiful or talented Holiday sister, but she had always been the most practical.

She sat up. "You know what? I'm not sorry I married Rome. I learned so much while living on the Remington Ranch. I learned I'm not a city girl. I'm a country girl. I love drafty houses with big porches and gardens filled with bright flowers and a barn filled with animals. Even if we lose the ranch, I'm going to find me and Mama, Daddy, and Mimi a house just like that. It might not be exactly like this one, or Rome's, but I can still make it a home."

That was the most important thing she'd learned from marrying Rome.

A house is only a home when you fill it with love.

The Holidays would always have plenty of that.

Much later in the day, that was confirmed when she walked in the house after Mimi had insisted she and Sweetie help her organize the gardening shed and discovered her entire family standing in the living room with big smiles on their faces and pointy birthday party hats on their heads. A banner that read, *Happy Birthday, Clover!* hung along the fireplace mantel and green and white streamers and balloons were everywhere.

"Surprise!"

Once again tears filled Cloe's eyes as her family surrounded her. Her birthday wasn't until tomorrow, but obviously they had wanted to surprise her. As she received hugs and birthday wishes, she realized she had so many things to be thankful for. She needed to stop moping around and start acting like it.

"Thank you so much," she said. "I have the best family in the world."

"Of course you do." Hallie hooked an arm through hers. "Now let's eat. I'm starving."

Her mama had made her favorite chicken pot-pie for dinner with German chocolate cake for dessert. As she blew out the candles, she had one wish . . . to celebrate the rest of her birthdays surrounded by her family.

Once the cake and ice cream had been eaten and Cloe finished opening her presents, Libby got up. "I think I'm going to take a walk and burn off some of these cake calories. Anyone want to join me?"

"I'll go." Decker started to stand, but Sweetie sent him a look that had him sitting back down. "Ahh, it's one of those secret sister moments."

Liberty glared at Sweetie and Sweetie held up her hands. "Don't look at me. You're the one who mentioned the Secret Sisterhood in front of him. But there's no need to worry. Our town sheriff knows how to keep a secret. Which is why I married him." She sent Decker a look as she got to her feet that could only be described as adoring. "Among other things."

Once the sisters were all gathered in the hayloft and Sweetie had brought the meeting to order, Liberty jumped right in.

"I won't let it happen! I won't let some asshole businessmen take our ranch! Especially after Cloe entered into a fake marriage to try and save it. Belle and I have planned parties for some of the most influential people in Houston. I'm sure they'll be happy to intervene on our behalf and make sure the owners of Oleander Investments pay for what they're trying to do."

"Amen to that," Hallie said with a fist punch. "We aren't going down without a fight."

"Calm down, y'all," Sweetie said. "I don't think we need to make Oleander Investments out like the bad guys. They made everything clear in the contract that Mimi signed. While she might not have known what she was signing, Daddy did. So we can't completely blame Corbin."

"He could have let Rome pay off the loan," Noelle said.

"Exactly!" Hallie piped up. "I'm glad Rome beat the tar out of that jackass at the Hellhole last night."

Cloe turned to her. "What?"

"You didn't hear? It's all over town. I heard it when I was getting gas in town. I guess Rome walked up and punched Corbin Whitlock right in the mouth. Then all hell broke loose and Decker got called."

"Decker?" Cloe looked at Sweetie. "You didn't tell me Decker got called to the Hellhole."

"I'm sorry," Sweetie said. "But I can't gossip about what Decker does as sheriff, Cloe. That's just not right."

"Corbin Whitlock?" Liberty looked at Belle. "Didn't we go to school with a Corbin Whitlock?"

Belle shook her head. "I'm sure it's not the same one."

"Oh, yes, it is," Hallie said. "It's the exact same one who went to school with y'all."

Belle looked as stunned as Cloe felt.

"Wait a second," Liberty said. "I remember him now. He had a major crush on me. He brought me wilted wildflowers and wrote me some pretty awful poems. But he *was* kind of sweet. For a while I actually considered dating him." She paused, her eyes narrowing. "In fact, I think he asked me out on a date. But for some reason, I didn't go."

"Maybe that's our in," Noelle said. "Maybe you can talk him into changing his mind about foreclosing on the ranch."

"No!" Belle burst out. When everyone turned to her, she blushed. "I mean I just don't think that it's a good idea. Look what happened to Cloe."

"I'm not planning on marrying him, Belly," Liberty said. "I'm just planning on reminding him we're old friends."

"I don't think you were ever friends, Libby."

"Maybe not. But by the time I get through with him, he'll think we are."

Cloe was with Belle. She didn't think it was a good idea for Liberty to meet with Corbin. Her sister had never known how to mince her words. But before she could give her opinion, she heard the sound of a truck pulling up to the front of the house. Noelle, who was sitting closest to the open hayloft doors, looked out.

"It's Rome."

Cloe's heart felt like it jumped straight into her throat. "Rome?" she croaked.

Hallie got up and looked out. "Yep. He just got out and is heading to the door. He's pulling a trailer. I wonder if he bought himself a new horse. Hey, Rome! Did you get yourself a new horse?"

"Don't call him over here!" Cloe snapped. Since she never snapped, all her sisters turned to her with surprise.

"Too late," Noelle said. "He's coming this way."

Cloe felt panicked. She couldn't see him. She wasn't ready to see him. "Don't tell him I'm here."

Again all her sisters looked at her with confusion. Everyone but Sweetie. She took Cloe's hand and squeezed it.

"You'll have to see him sooner or later."

"What's going on?" Liberty said. "Why is Cloe so upset about seeing Rome? I thought their marriage was—"

"Hey, Hallie." Rome's deep voice carried up through the open doors of the loft and cut Liberty off. "Is Cloe around?"

Hallie, bless her heart, had always been good at lying. "Nope. She went to town. So did you get a new horse?"

"No. We've had Lady Grantham for a while now. But she's been missing Cloe pretty badly so I figured she'd be happier here."

Noelle looked at Cloe with wide eyes and spoke loud enough to be heard in two counties. "He brought you a horse!"

Hallie turned to Noelle and rolled her eyes before she looked at Cloe for direction. Sweetie made the decision for her.

"Come on, y'all. Let's let Cloe and Rome have a few minutes alone."

All her sisters got to their feet, but Liberty didn't head for the ladder. "Before I leave, I'd like to know what's going on."

Belle took her arm. "I'm sure Cloe will tell us when she's ready. Right now, she has a horse to thank Rome for."

"Hell yeah, she does," Hallie said. "If a man brought me a horse, I'd thank the hell out of him."

Once they were gone, Cloe got up and moved to the open hatch. Rome stood directly below, the crown of his Stetson and his broad shoulders all she could see. He greeted her sisters as they came out of the barn and exchanged pleasantries with them. It was only after they headed to the house that he finally glanced up.

Just the sight of his face made Cloe's eyes swim in tears. There was no way to blink them back or keep the tremble out of her voice.

"I can't accept Lady Grantham."

His gaze trapped her in soft gray that match the twilight sky. In those eyes, she saw something that made her breath catch and her heart warm.

"What about your husband? Will you accept me?"

CHAPTER TWENTY

ROME DIDN'T WAIT for Cloe to answer. He had prepared a speech and he knew he needed to get it out before he lost his nerve. His stomach already felt like it was filled with Mexican jumping beans. His heart just felt tight and scared.

He swept off his hat and cleared his throat. "As you know, I'm pretty screwed up where love is concerned. I told you I didn't trust love. And I still don't. But as it turns out you don't have to trust love to fall in love. I fell in love with you, Cloe Holiday. I fell in love with your kindness and the way you open your heart to everyone you meet. I fell in love with your laughter and I'll do just about anything to see your dimples flash. I fell in love with your passion for everything you undertake—cooking, gardening, riding, fixing up the house . . . making love. We did make love, Cloe. And it scared me. It scared the hell out of me. Because I knew it wasn't just physical. I knew my heart was involved the entire time we touched and held each other. I was afraid of getting that heart broken if you left. And you did leave. And guess what? My heart is broken."

He could see the tears rolling down her cheeks. He wanted nothing more than to hold her and wipe each and every one away and never make her cry again. But he had learned the hard way that wasn't how love worked. Love was tears and laughter and pain and joy all wrapped up in a big ol' messy bundle. As much as you might want to open that bundle and only take what you wanted, you couldn't.

It was all or nothing.

He wanted it all. The tears and pain and laughter and joy. The fear . . . and hope.

Now all he had to do was convince Cloe.

"I don't care about the land. The land wasn't the reason I married you, Cloe. It was the excuse my subconscious came up with to get what it wanted. You. I think I wanted you from the moment you took my hand during my panic attack. From that moment on, you became my lifeline—the lucky charm who brought joy back into my life. And I don't want to lose you . . . please don't let me lose you."

He dropped to one knee and pulled out the ring box he'd had in his pocket since buying it this morning. Casey had gone with him to Austin and wanted him to buy the biggest diamond in the jewelry store. But Rome knew that wasn't Cloe's style. She was subtle, but amazing and unique. Which is why he didn't buy her a diamond at all.

He bought her an emerald that matched her eyes.

Eyes that now glittered with tears.

"Will you marry me, Lucky? For real, this time."

She stared at him for what felt like eternity before she disappeared. Another eternity passed before she came flying out the open barn door and hurled herself at him. He dropped his hat and the ring to catch her, but since he was only balancing on one knee, he ended up flat on his back with Cloe lying on top of him.

Her eyes twinkled and her smile was so big her dimples looked twice as deep as she looked down at him. "And you thought you weren't good at poetry, Romeo."

One month later, Roman Samuel Remington found himself in a tuxedo standing at an altar once again. But this time, there were no bad memories or panic attacks . . . although his heart did almost beat out of his chest as he watched Cloe walking down the aisle toward him.

Since this was more of a celebration than a wedding, there was no traditional white dress and veil. Instead, her dress was a deep vibrant green that matched her eyes and showed off her long legs. The wispy material clung to her full breasts and flared out around her slim hips. One of her sisters had fixed her hair and it hung past her shoulders in a wealth of flaming burgundy curls that begged to be touched. Spring flowers of every color encircled her head and she looked like the most stunningly beautiful rainbow he'd ever seen in his life.

She was his rainbow. He knew as long as she was beside him, his life would be a pot of gold. When she reached him, he waited for her to hand her bouquet to Sweetie before he took her hands in his.

"Hey, Lucky."

She smiled and her dimples flashed. "This is a little different than the first time, isn't it?"

He grinned. It was a lot different. They were standing in the Holiday Ranch barn surrounded by most of the town. Her sisters had decorated the inside of the barn in all shades of spring colors. Outside the open doors, the shades of spring continued. The sun was shining and the daffodils and tulips in Mimi's garden were blooming. It was indicative of the way he felt. The winter of his heart was over and spring had arrived.

"This wedding isn't completely different from the first time," he said. "Even then, I was trying to get your attention."

She squeezed his hands. "You've always held my attention, Rome. I just never thought I could hold yours."

"You hold it, Clover Fields. You hold it, along with my heart, forever."

Her eyes welled with tears. "Forever."

Even though he wasn't supposed to kiss Cloe until after they'd renewed their vows with the town preacher, he couldn't wait. He pulled her into his arms and kissed her. For a moment, the world disappeared and it was just him and the woman in his arms.

Then hooting and applause filtered in and he pulled back to see the townsfolk beaming. That was one thing about a small town—they had no problem changing their views.

"I knew it was a match made in heaven from the start," seemed to be the catchphrase for the reception. Not one person mentioned the betting pool. Mrs. Stokes did however slip him a wad of cash during the dollar dance and said, "I knew you two were a sure bet."

Something that *was* talked about at the reception was the Holidays losing their ranch. Overnight, Corbin Whitlock had become the villain of Wilder, Texas, and was now referred to as Corbin Whiplash after the villainous cartoon character Snidely Whiplash.

Rome still intended to do all he could to keep Corbin from foreclosing on the Holiday Ranch. But he wasn't going to worry about that tonight. Tonight, he had one goal.

Make his bride smile.

She *did* smile. She smiled all through dinner and the cutting of the cheesecake Noelle had made and her dance with her father and her and Rome's first dance together. But she stopped smiling after their third two-step and he noticed she'd grown pale.

He studied her with concern. "Are you okay?"

She shook her head. "I think I need to take a break."

"I have the perfect place." He led her to the hayloft ladder.

He had asked Liberty and Belle to set it up for him and he had to give Cloe's sisters kudos when he got to the loft and saw what they'd done. There weren't just a couple lanterns, a comforter, and some champagne. The entire loft was filled with twinkle lights—the rafters, the bales of hay, all along the open hatch door. In front of those doors, the pile of hay had been turned into a sultan's bed with a puffy satin comforter and piles of coordinating throw pillows. Next to it was a silver ice bucket with a bottle of champagne and fluted glasses . . . along with a silver tray of chocolate-covered strawberries.

"Oh my gosh." Cloe held a hand to her chest and turned to him. "Did you do this?"

"I asked Liberty and Belle to." He looked up at the rafters covered in twinkle lights. "But I didn't think they'd go to such extremes."

"Then you don't know my sisters." She leaned in and kissed his cheek. "Thank you for making us a love nest."

He pulled her into his arms. "I have fond memories of this hayloft. It's where I first got a glimpse of the real Cloe."

She drew back. "A rambling drunk?"

He gently pushed her glasses back up on her nose before he kissed the tip. "A woman who cares so much for her family she didn't want them to know how much she was hurting. I don't want you to do that with me, Cloe. If you're upset about something, I want to know it. Now tell me what's wrong. You have been acting a little strange all day. Are you worried about the ranch? Or is it something else? Come on, Lucky. You can tell me anything."

She hesitated for only a second. "I'm pregnant." Before he could get over his shock, she burst out in tears.

His heart took flight with joy and, at the same time, felt like it would break from seeing her so upset. Not knowing what to do, he pulled her into his arms and held her tight. "Oh, Cloe, don't cry. I thought you wanted kids."

She shook her head against his chest and spoke with heart-wrenching sobs. "No—it's not—that. It's just—the opposite. I've always wanted kids and to find a man who would love me, but I thought I wasn't going to get it all." She hiccupped. "But here I am, the least likely Holiday sister to get everything—and I got everything!"

Relief filled him and he drew back and cupped her face in his hands, his thumbs brushing away her tears. "You deserve everything, Cloe. You've always put your family first. It's time that you were first. But I know exactly what you mean. I thought I didn't deserve everything either. But I guess it's not about what you deserve. It's about what you open yourself up to. I'm sure glad I opened my heart to you, Clover Fields Holiday. A baby?" The joy he felt had him releasing a whoop as he lifted her off her feet and swung her around.

She laughed. "So I guess you're happy with the news. And it's not Clover Fields Holiday any more. It's Clover Fields Remington from now on, thank you very much."

A smile broke over his face as he set her on her feet. "Damn straight it is. Of course I'm happy about the baby." He placed his hand on her stomach. "I want this child and I want as many children as you want to give me."

Her dimples flashed. "How about six?"

He answered her smile. "That's always seemed like the perfect number to me. My daddy is going to be over the moon. But you should have told me sooner."

"I wasn't sure until this morning when I took the pregnancy test that Mimi gave me."

"Mimi?"

Cloe nodded. "She told me a week ago that I was pregnant. I thought it was just her wishful thinking, but I humored her anyway. It turns out, she was right."

Rome laughed. "Of course she was. The woman is rarely wrong. Which makes me wonder if she won't figure out a way to keep the ranch."

"You might be right. Especially when Liberty has decided she's coming home to take on Corbin Whitlock and Oleander Investments. I'm pretty sure all hell is about to break loose."

Since Rome had lost his own temper with the owner of Oleander Investments, he couldn't say anything about Liberty losing hers. But when Cloe yawned widely, he put aside all thoughts of losing the Holiday Ranch and led her over to the sultan's bed.

Once he made sure she was comfortable, he

took off his Stetson and tuxedo jacket and joined her, spooning around her just like he'd done only months before. Only this time, his hand rested on her stomach.

"A baby." He kissed the top of her head. "And to think that it all started right here."

She cuddled closer, her bottom pushing into his lap and making him instantly hard. "That morning I woke up in your arms, my body knew I was exactly where I was supposed to be. I've never felt so content."

"I felt the same way."

"No, you didn't. You had a major hard-on."

"Only after I realized my hand was tucked so sweetly between your boobs." He slipped his hand over one abundant breast and gently squeezed.

She giggled. "You're shameless."

"You want to see how shameless we can be?" he whispered in her ear as he lifted the hem of her dress.

Much later, when they were both sated, he glanced out the open hayloft door. The sun had set and twilight turned the sky to a hazy midnight blue. One star twinkled on the horizon. "So should we make a wish?" he asked.

"There's no need." Her smile when she looked up at him was as brilliant as the star. "From now on, just call me Lucky."

THE END

Turn the page for a SNEAK PEEK of the next Holiday Ranch romance!

SNEAK PEEK

WRANGLING A TEXAS FIRECRACKER!
Coming April 2024!

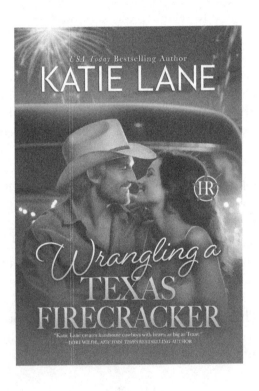

CHAPTER ONE

FOUR HUNDRED AND fifty-three wooly sheep later, Liberty Lou Holiday was still wide-awake.

She wanted to blame her sleeplessness on being in the country. After living in an apartment in downtown Houston for the last five years, she was used to the sounds of a big city: Bustling traffic, blaring sirens, and partying neighbors. She was no longer used to the creaks and hums of the old farmhouse she had grown up in. Or the chirp and buzz of the insect band that had positioned itself beneath her open window. But the truth was that it wasn't the cricket quartet or the creaks of the old farmhouse keeping her awake.

To Liberty, sleep was a waste of time. She would much rather be answering emails, uploading photographs from the last wedding on the Holiday Sisters Events website, posting on their social media pages, and maybe even watching some TikTok for event ideas. Unfortunately, the wi-fi at the ranch had gone out that morning and the wi-fi company couldn't send someone out until the following week.

So here she was, staring at the One Direction poster on the ceiling of her childhood bedroom and counting an entire flock of sheep. Maybe that was her problem. As a cattle rancher's daughter, maybe she shouldn't be counting sheep. Maybe she should be counting cows.

Not that her father owned cows anymore. All the cattle had been sold to pay off the ranch's debt. It still hadn't been enough to save the Holiday Ranch from foreclosure.

A few weeks ago, Liberty had wanted to hogtie the owner of Oleander Investments, the company who was foreclosing on the ranch, string him up in the old oak tree in the backyard, and take turns with her five sisters beating him with a piñata stick. But after she learned he was the sweet boy she'd gone to high school with, her temper had cooled.

Corbin Whitlock wasn't the type of person to kick a family out of their home. He probably didn't even know the Holiday Ranch was being foreclosed on. Oleander was a large company and things happened in a large company that bosses weren't always aware of. Holiday Sisters Events was a small business and there were still things that slipped past Liberty. Thankfully, she had her twin sister, Belle, to catch those little details.

Liberty was sure as soon as Corbin found out who the ranch belonged to he would stop the foreclosure proceedings immediately. He'd had a crush on Liberty in high school. When she met with him tomorrow morning, she intended to be the charming head cheerleader, homecoming queen, and student council president of all his adolescent dreams.

That was if she didn't have big bags under her eyes from lack of sleep.

Maybe what she needed to get to sleep wasn't sheep as much as exercise.

Tossing back the covers, she sat up and reached for her old roper cowboy boots. The leather was so soft and worn they molded to her feet like a cozy pair of slippers. In Houston, she wore designer high heels that added a good four inches to her already tall five-foot-nine-inch height. But here on the ranch, there were no snobby socialites she needed to impress—no arrogant businessmen she needed to intimidate.

Not wanting to wake her mama, daddy, and Grandma Mimi, she decided to exit the house the same way she had as a teenager. But climbing out the two-story window and down from the oak tree had been much easier when she'd been younger. Or maybe what had been easier was doing it in jeans versus a skimpy tank top and a pair of baggy boxers. By the time she finally made it to the ground, she had bark-scraps on the back of her thighs and a splinter in her butt.

After picking out the splinter, she headed toward the barn that sat behind the house. It was the quintessential country barn—big and red with a hayloft over the wide double doors. Just looking at it brought back sweet memories of grooming beloved horses, playing with litters of kittens and baby farm animals, having secret sister meetings in the hayloft, and, recently, hosting two weddings.

It was still hard to believe that Sweetie and Cloe were married . . . and that Cloe was now pregnant with Liberty's first niece or nephew. Just the thought of a sweet little baby caused her heart to clench with longing, but she had never been one to wallow in self-pity so she doused the feeling with a good dose of logic. She didn't have time for marriage or kids. Her entire focus should be on turning Holiday Sisters Events into the most successful event planning business in all of Texas. She and Belle were well on their way to making that dream come true. Their calendar was filled all the way until next year with weddings, anniversary and birthday parties, and business and holiday events.

Which was why it was so hard being here when she should be back in Houston working along side Belle. But all six of the Holiday sisters had agreed to take a shift staying at the farmhouse to help their parents and grandmother unravel the mess their daddy had made of the ranch's finances and help them through the process of losing the land that had been in her family for generations. Sweetie and Cloe had taken their turns and now it was Liberty's. Instead of bellyaching about it, she needed to concentrate on doing everything she could to keep her family from losing their house too.

And this barn.

After putting together two weddings for her sisters, Liberty had come to realize what a gold mine the barn was. It was a perfect wedding venue. She'd had more than a few clients who had wanted a country-themed wedding and would have loved having their wedding and reception in a barn—even if it was over an hour away from Houston. But since barn venues were snatched up quickly, they'd had to settle for a hotel reception with bales of hay and country decorations.

But if Liberty could convince a sweet country boy to not foreclose on her family's ranch, her new brother-in-law, Rome Remington, would pay off the loan in exchange for the land and Holiday Ranch would stay in the family. Mama, Daddy, and Mimi would get to keep the house and barn.

A barn that would become extremely profitable if Liberty had anything to say about it.

As Liberty stood there looking at the barn and thinking about how much money she could make on it, a soft breeze blew over her, bringing with it the familiar scent of Texas wildflowers.

While she'd been born in the middle of summer, springtime was her favorite time in Texas. The winds were mild and the humidity low with temperatures usually in the high seventies or low eighties. Everywhere you looked, wildflowers bloomed in a rainbow of colors. Being that it was late April, the bluebonnets were gone, but primrose, poppies, Indian paintbrush, and phlox were in full bloom. The moon hung in the clear night sky like a relaxing C and clusters of stars twinkled like sequins on a prom dress.

As much as she hated to admit it, Liberty had

KATIE LANE

missed home. She had missed the wide-open spaces and the scent of rich earth and cow manure. She had missed the sky that stretched from horizon to horizon without one building or billboard to block the view.

Making her way around the barn, she headed across the open pasture. She didn't pay attention to where she was going, but somehow her feet knew. Before long, she reached a cluster of oaks, mesquite, and Cyprus trees.

Cooper Springs had always been one of her favorite spots on the ranch. In the very center of the trees was a crystal clear pool of water that held memories of picnics with her family, skinny-dipping with her sisters, and fishing with her daddy. The clear blue water looked magical with the moon and stars reflected in its surface.

She didn't hesitate to slip off her boots and dip her toes in.

The water was cold, but not too cold. After the long walk, it felt good. She stripped off her tank and boxers and dove in. The shock of the cold water took her breath away and she came up gasping. Her gasp turned to a startled shriek when a deep voice spoke behind her.

"It shore takes your breath away, don't it, darlin'?"

She whirled to see a man treading water not more than ten feet away. It was too dark to see the features of his face. All she could make out was the dark outline of his broad shoulders and the golden-red tint of his slicked back hair. Once she got over her surprise, annoyance set in.

"This is private property. You have exactly ten seconds to get gone or I'm calling the sheriff—who just happens to be my brother-in-law and lives right down that road."

There wasn't a speck of concern in his reply. Just humor. "I hate to doubt a lady, but I am a little curious about how you plan on calling your big bad sheriff brother-in-law. Because if my eyes didn't deceive me—and they rarely do when I'm truly focused on something—you aren't carrying a cellphone."

Most women would be a little intimidated about now. It was dark. He was a stranger. She was alone . . . and naked. But Liberty wasn't most women. She had a drawer of first place ribbons in both the breaststroke and the hundred-yard dash. She knew she could outswim and outrun this cocky man with both hands tied behind her back.

She stared him down. "I don't need a cellphone when I was voted loudest cheerleader ever to grace the halls of Wilder High. Leave now or I'll make sure people hear me scream in the next county."

He held up his hands, moonlight reflecting off a pair of extremely well developed biceps. "Now don't get all riled, darlin'. I'm not here to cause any trouble. I heard how pretty Cooper Springs is and had to see it for myself." He lowered his hands and continued to tread. "I also heard that this property no longer belongs to the Holidays. And I'm assuming you're a Holiday."

Damn, the townsfolk of Wilder. They never had

known when to keep their big mouths shut. "Yes, I'm a Holiday and you've heard wrong. Possession is nine-tenths the law. And as long as my family is still living on this ranch, these springs are ours."

"That's not quite how the law works, but I'm not here to argue over who does and does not own these springs." He glanced around. "There seems to be plenty of space for two insomniacs to enjoy a late night swim. I'm Jesse Cates, by the way. A mediocre rodeo roper and a restless wanderlust."

"So, basically, you're a rodeo bum."

His teeth flashed. "Pretty much. And you are?" When she started to answer, he cut her off. "No, wait. Let me guess. You're one of the infamous Holiday sisters. Since I heard Sweetheart and Clover are married and you don't seem to have a husband in tow, I'm going to say you're either Liberty, Belle, Halloween, or Noelle. Since I also heard that Belle and Liberty live in Houston and Noelle in Dallas, I'm going to have to go with Halloween. Or Hallie, as I hear you prefer to be called. And I can't very well blame you. I love the holiday, but sure wouldn't want to be named after it."

Liberty didn't correct him. "It sounds like the townsfolk have been running off at the mouth."

"What can I say? I have a way of putting people at ease. It's my face. Red hair and freckles aren't what you'd call threatening. If you could see it, you wouldn't be at all worried about sharing your springs with Opie Taylor." He pleaded.

"Come on. Let me stay. I give you my word I'll keep my distance. I just need to get rid of some pent up energy."

Since Liberty knew all about having too much energy, she understood his dilemma. "Fine. But get too close and I swear I'll scream these trees down."

Again, his smile flashed. "I believe it." With only a slight hesitation, he dipped under the water and started to do laps. She joined him, but kept on her side of the springs.

He was a good swimmer. His strokes were strong and consistent. Which made her swim faster. But just as she started to pass him, he moved ahead again. It wasn't a race, but it sure as hell felt like one. Liberty wasn't about to let him beat her or outlast her. Even though her lungs burned and her muscles had started to cramp, she swam like she was swimming for the gold. But every time she started to pull ahead, he caught up. She got the distinct feeling he was toying with her.

Which really annoyed her.

At the opposite shore, she stopped swimming and came up for air. He went only a few strokes further before he too stopped. During the swim, they had gotten closer. Liberty realized it had more to do with her than with him. He had stayed on his side, while she had been the one who had edged over in his lane. This close, his shoulders looked even broader and his biceps even bigger. It was still too dark to see his features clearly, but she could tell he was handsome with a strong jaw and that cocky smile.

"I won," he said in his thick east Texas drawl.

"I wasn't racing," she lied.

"Sure you weren't."

It annoyed her that he read her so easily. "I wasn't. If I had been, you wouldn't stand a chance."

"Then let's go again." She started to decline, but he added. "Unless you're not up for the challenge."

Even though her lungs still burned and her muscles felt like they had been wrung through her great-grandmother's antique washing machine, Liberty had never been able to ignore a challenge. "Oh, I'm up for it. But a challenge isn't a challenge without a reward. Twenty bucks says I'll beat that cocky grin off your face. Unless that's too much for a rodeo bum."

The cocky grin got even bigger. "Actually, I was thinking more of a hundred."

She snorted. "As if you have a hundred."

He stared back at her, his eyes dark and intense. "In the pocket of my jeans lying right over there by that tree, darlin'."

"Fine," she said. "A hundred it is."

"And you have a hundred with you?"

"Well, no. But I'm good for it."

"I'm not saying you aren't a woman of your word, but you can't bet something you don't have. I have a hundred so I can bet a hundred. What do you have?"

"I don't usually bring money with me when I go for midnight swims."

"Then you'll have to bet something else against my hundred."

"Like what?"

He hesitated for only a second before he spoke. "How about a kiss?"

Order
**Wrangling a
Texas Firecracker**
Today!
http://tinyurl.com/m5ab4epz
Or
www.katielanebooks.com

Also by Katie Lane

Be sure to check out all of Katie Lane's novels!
www.katielanebooks.com

Holiday Ranch Series
Wrangling a Texas Sweetheart
Wrangling a Lucky Cowboy
Wrangling a Texas Firecracker—April 2024

Kingman Ranch Series
Charming a Texas Beast
Charming a Knight in Cowboy Boots
Charming a Big Bad Texan
Charming a Fairytale Cowboy
Charming a Texas Prince
Charming a Christmas Texan
Charming a Cowboy King

Bad Boy Ranch Series:
Taming a Texas Bad Boy
Taming a Texas Rebel
Taming a Texas Charmer
Taming a Texas Heartbreaker
Taming a Texas Devil
Taming a Texas Rascal
Taming a Texas Tease
Taming a Texas Christmas Cowboy

Brides of Bliss Texas Series:
Spring Texas Bride
Summer Texas Bride
Autumn Texas Bride
Christmas Texas Bride

Tender Heart Texas Series:
Falling for Tender Heart
Falling Head Over Boots
Falling for a Texas Hellion
Falling for a Cowboy's Smile
Falling for a Christmas Cowboy

Deep in the Heart of Texas Series:
Going Cowboy Crazy
Make Mine a Bad Boy
Catch Me a Cowboy
Trouble in Texas
Flirting with Texas
A Match Made in Texas
The Last Cowboy in Texas
My Big Fat Texas Wedding

Overnight Billionaires Series:
A Billionaire Between the Sheets
A Billionaire After Dark
Waking up with a Billionaire

Hunk for the Holidays Series:
Hunk for the Holidays
Ring in the Holidays
Unwrapped

ABOUT THE AUTHOR

KATIE LANE IS a firm believer that love conquers alKatie Lane is a firm believer that love conquers all and laughter is the best medicine. Which is why you'll find plenty of humor and happily-ever-afters in her contemporary and western contemporary romance novels. A USA Today Bestselling Author, she has written numerous series, including *Deep in the Heart of Texas, Hunk for the Holidays, Overnight Billionaires, Tender Heart Texas, The Brides of Bliss Texas, Bad Boy Ranch, Kingman Ranch,* and *Holiday Ranch*. Katie lives in Albuquerque, New Mexico, and when she's not writing, she enjoys reading, eating chocolate (dark, please), and snuggling with her high school sweetheart and cairn terrier, Roo.

For more on her writing life or just to chat, check out Katie here:
FACEBOOK
www.facebook.com/katielaneauthor
INSTAGRAM
www.instagram.com/katielanebooks.

And for more information on upcoming releases and great giveaways, be sure to sign up for her mailing list at www.katielanebooks.com!

Made in the USA
Monee, IL
20 February 2024

53822410R00144